BARRON'S BOOK NOTES

H

For Whom the Bell Tolls

BARRON'S BOOK NOTES

ERNEST HEMINGWAY'S

For Whom the Bell Tolls

BY

Jim Auer

SERIES COORDINATOR
Murray Bromberg
Principal, Wang High School of Queens
Holliswood, New York

Past President
High School Principals Association of New York City

BARRON'S

BARRON'S EDUCATIONAL SERIES, INC.

All inquiries should be addressed to:
Barron's Educational Series, Inc.
113 Crossways Park Drive
Woodbury, New York 11797

Library of Congress Catalog Card No. 85-3944

International Standard Book No. 0-8120-3515-1

Library of Congress Cataloging in Publication Data
Auer, Jim.
  Ernest Hemingway's For whom the bell tolls.

  (Barron's book notes)
  Bibliography: p. 126
  Summary: A guide to reading "For Whom the Bell Tolls"
with a critical and appreciative mind encouraging analysis
of plot, style, form, and structure. Also includes
background on the author's life and times, sample tests,
term paper suggestions, and a reading list.
    1. Hemingway, Ernest, 1899–1961. For whom the bell
tolls. [1. Hemingway, Ernest, 1899–1961. For whom the
bell tolls. 2. American literature—History and
criticism] I. Title. II. Series.
PS3515.E37F7323 1986   813'.52   85-3944
ISBN 0-8120-3515-1

PRINTED IN THE UNITED STATES OF AMERICA

3 4   550   98765432

CONTENTS

ADVISORY BOARD

We wish to thank the following educators who helped us focus our *Book Notes* series to meet student needs and critiqued our manuscripts to provide quality materials.

Sandra Dunn, English Teacher
Hempstead High School, Hempstead, New York

Lawrence J. Epstein, Associate Professor of English
Suffolk County Community College, Selden, New York

Leonard Gardner, Lecturer, English Department
State University of New York at Stony Brook

Beverly A. Haley, Member, Advisory Committee
National Council of Teachers of English Student
Guide Series, Fort Morgan, Colorado

Elaine C. Johnson, English Teacher
Tamalpais Union High School District
Mill Valley, California

Marvin J. LaHood, Professor of English
State University of New York College at Buffalo

Robert Lecker, Associate Professor of English
McGill University, Montréal, Québec, Canada

David E. Manly, Professor of Educational Studies
State University of New York College at Geneseo

Bruce Miller, Associate Professor of Education
State University of New York at Buffalo

Frank O'Hare, Professor of English and
Director of Writing
Ohio State University, Columbus, Ohio

Faith Z. Schullstrom, Member, Executive Committee
National Council of Teachers of English
Director of Curriculum and Instruction
Guilderland Central School District, New York

Mattie C. Williams, Director, Bureau of Language Arts
Chicago Public Schools, Chicago, Illinois

HOW TO USE THIS BOOK

You have to know how to approach literature in order to get the most out of it. This *Barron's Book Notes* volume follows a plan based on methods used by some of the best students to read a work of literature.

Begin with the guide's section on the author's life and times. As you read, try to form a clear picture of the author's personality, circumstances, and motives for writing the work. This background usually will make it easier for you to hear the author's tone of voice, and follow where the author is heading.

Then go over the rest of the introductory material—such sections as those on the plot, characters, setting, themes, and style of the work. Underline, or write down in your notebook, particular things to watch for, such as contrasts between characters and repeated literary devices. At this point, you may want to develop a system of symbols to use in marking your text as you read. (Of course, you should only mark up a book you own, not one that belongs to another person or a school.) Perhaps you will want to use a different letter for each character's name, a different number for each major theme of the book, a different color for each important symbol or literary device. Be prepared to mark up the pages of your book as you read. Put your marks in the margins so you can find them again easily.

Now comes the moment you've been waiting for— the time to start reading the work of literature. You may want to put aside your *Barron's Book Notes* volume until you've read the work all the way through. Or you may want to alternate, reading the *Book Notes* analysis of each section as soon as you have finished reading the corresponding part of the original. Before you move on, reread crucial passages you don't fully understand. (Don't take this guide's analysis for granted—make up your own mind as to what the work means.)

Once you've finished the whole work of literature, you may want to review it right away, so you can firm up your ideas about what it means. You may want to leaf through the book concentrating on passages you marked in reference to one character or one theme. This is also a good time to reread the *Book Notes* introductory material, which pulls together insights on specific topics.

When it comes time to prepare for a test or to write a paper, you'll already have formed ideas about the work. You'll be able to go back through it, refreshing your memory as to the author's exact words and perspective, so that you can support your opinions with evidence drawn straight from the work. Patterns will emerge, and ideas will fall into place; your essay question or term paper will almost write itself. Give yourself a dry run with one of the sample tests in the guide. These tests present both multiple-choice and essay questions. An accompanying section gives answers to the multiple-choice questions as well as suggestions for writing the essays. If you have to select a term paper topic, you may choose one from the list of suggestions in this book. This guide also provides you with a reading list, to help you when you start research for a term paper, and a selection of provocative comments by critics, to spark your thinking before you write.

THE AUTHOR
AND HIS TIMES

In June 1937, Ernest Hemingway addressed the Second Congress of American Writers at Carnegie Hall in New York City. His subject was the Spanish Civil War, which had started in 1936 and which he had observed first-hand for some months as a correspondent of the North American Newspaper Alliance. In his speech, which was warmly received by the audience, Hemingway spoke of his deep hatred for the fascist forces trying to overthrow the Republican government in Spain, particularly for the way they suppressed artists, notably writers.

"Really good writers are always rewarded under almost any existing system of government that they can tolerate," Hemingway said in his speech. "There is only one form of government that cannot produce good writers, and that system is fascism. For fascism is a lie told by bullies. A writer who will not lie cannot live and work under fascism."

Hemingway's apparent devotion to the Republican cause in this war was greeted with cheers by liberals in the United States. Here was Ernest Hemingway, a famous novelist, declaring his allegiance to their cause! His pledge of support seemed particularly welcome, since he had long resisted public political commitment of any kind and had been criticized for his reluctance to become involved in the important issues of the day. Now he had thrown himself into the midst of the controversy.

Hemingway returned to Spain to watch the battle rage, and he became increasingly frustrated by the failure of the Republicans to hold their own against the fascist rebels. He was also sickened by the corruption and ineptness of Republicans and Nationalists alike. He called this situation "the carnival of treachery and rottenness on both sides," and was especially critical of the military leaders. Hemingway decided that he could best serve the Republican cause by writing about the war as honestly as possible. "The hell with war for awhile," he said, "I want to write." The result of his creative urge was the novel *For Whom the Bell Tolls*, which was published in 1940, the year after the Republicans had lost the war.

* * *

For someone who lived his adult years with bold, muscular strokes in public view across three continents, Hemingway's early life was relatively uneventful. He was born in Oak Park, Illinois, a suburb of Chicago, on July 21, 1899. His mother was artistic and cultured, and might have followed a career as an opera singer. She tried to urge Ernest to develop musical inclinations, but with no results. His great love was the outdoors, the appreciation of which he learned from his father, a physician, who relished fishing, hunting, and the lore of the woods. Ernest acquired ideals of endurance, physical prowess, and courage that later show up in his writing and his life.

When he was graduated from high school in 1917, Hemingway had no desire to go to college. His interest was World War I, which had been raging for three years. He wanted to participate before the fighting ended, but he was met by disappointment. At first Hemingway's father refused to let him enlist, and when his father finally relented, the American armed forces rejected Hemingway for poor vision in one eye.

Hemingway then worked as a reporter for the Kansas City *Star* for six months until he found a way to participate in the war—as an ambulance driver with the American Red Cross. By June 1918 he was at the front lines in Italy. During a furious Austrian shelling of Italian troops, he carried a wounded soldier to safety, but was struck along the way by pieces of mortar shrapnel.

The Italian government decorated Hemingway for his heroism, newspapers printed glowing stories, and a hero's welcome awaited him in Oak Park. But Hemingway was nonetheless plagued by rejection in other areas: He had fallen in love with Agnes von Kurowsky, a nurse who had cared for him in an Italian hospital, but in 1919 she broke off their relationship. And his determination to be a writer was dampened by rejection slips from one magazine after another.

Coloring almost everything was his disillusionment with the values he had learned while growing up. His experience in the war overseas had changed his outlook, and he became more and more estranged from his parents. In Europe he encountered cynicism about the war, not patriotism, and there was an overwhelming loss of hope and belief in traditional values.

In September 1921, Hemingway married Hadley Richardson. The couple moved to Paris, where Hemingway served as a correspondent for *The Toronto Star*. Paris was a gathering place for American expatriates—people who chose to live away from their homeland, mostly because they were disillusioned or confused about their lives and their country. One writer dubbed these rootless people "the lost generation."

Hemingway's desire to be a full-time writer of fiction was still unfulfilled. Manuscript after manuscript was turned down by publishers. Another devastating blow came in December 1923 when a suitcase containing almost everything he had written was stolen and never recovered.

But in 1924 a small collection of his short stories, *in our time*, was published in Paris. In 1925, retitled with capitals, *In Our Time* was published in the United States and ultimately received high critical praise. His terse, direct style (developed in part by his need to use as few words as possible as a foreign correspondent) and his ability to articulate intense, complex emotions without flowery excess, was greeted with warm welcome by many critics, who saw him as helping initiate a departure from the verbal indulgences of many writers of the 19th century. Hemingway further polished his style in his first novel, *The Sun Also Rises* (1926). The book, a telling depiction of life among American expatriates in Europe, was warmly received by both critics and the reading public.

In 1927, Hemingway divorced Hadley and married Pauline Pfeiffer, a writer for *Vogue* magazine. They moved to Key West, Florida, where he worked on *A Farewell to Arms* (1929) and Pauline gave birth to the first of their two sons. Just as he was completing the final draft of *A Farewell to Arms*, which would bring him even more critical and financial success, he learned that his father—despondent and ill with diabetes—had shot himself to death. Hemingway considered suicide a cowardly act, and never forgave his father for it. Yet the suicide would ultimately have a grim echo in Hemingway's own life.

The 1930s brought Hemingway adventure and broad, bold experiences. He indulged his love for deep-sea fishing off the coast of Florida and hunting in the American West and Africa. Always seeking intense physical experience, Hemingway spoke with awe about the thrill of the "clean kill." He wrote many magazine articles that glorified these brawny adventures, until the public generally identified him with the image of the hearty and rugged outdoorsman. Hemingway wrote two nonfiction books during this period, *Death in the Afternoon* (1932), which honored the ritual of the bullfight, and *Green Hills of Africa* (1935), detailing the glory of an African safari.

The Great Depression and other world problems helped develop a new side of Hemingway. Because the heroes in Hemingway's novels had been loners, independent and aloof from the problems of the masses, the generally left-leaning writers of the time disdained him and his outlook. That's one major reason why Hemingway was cheered so heartily in his address in 1937 to the Congress of American Writers: this was a new, politically committed Ernest Hemingway!

Hemingway's zeal for the Republican, or Loyalist, cause was revealed in actions as well as words. He accompanied both regular Republican army groups and guerrilla bands as a correspondent. He spent time in the Spanish cities, in the countryside, in the mountains. He also bought ambulances for the Loyalists, and helped prepare a pro-Loyalist documentary film, *The Spanish Earth*.

There was another aspect of Hemingway that

lured him to the scene of battle—his love of conflict itself. It would be simplistic to say that Hemingway glorified war, as some have charged. He was as sickened by its cruelty and waste as anyone could be. Yet he was also excited by what he saw as the more positive aspects of battle—courage, camaraderie, loyalty, dedication to a cause. According to one observer, Hemingway was "attracted by danger, death, great deeds"; another said he was "revived and rejuvenated" by seeing those who refused to surrender, no matter what the odds. Hemingway was also buoyed by what he called "the pleasant, comforting stench of comrades" fighting together for a common goal. Instincts similar to those that drew him to a bullfight or to the stalking of wild game sharpened his senses during the Spanish Civil War.

It is the conflicting impulses of attraction and repulsion that create much of the tension in *For Whom the Bell Tolls*. The publication of the novel was greeted with acclaim by some, but with disdain by others. Some liberals and some conservatives were angered because they felt Hemingway had betrayed them by not writing a novel that favored their respective political outlook. But Hemingway responded, "In stories about the war I try to show all the different sides of it, taking it slowly and honestly and examining it in many ways. So never think one story represents my viewpoint because it is much too complicated for that."

For Whom the Bell Tolls was a great commercial success. Paramount Pictures acquired the film rights for $150,000, an astronomical sum at the time. Hemingway stipulated who the principal actors should be—the very popular Gary Cooper would be Robert Jordan, the main figure in the novel, and the rising star Ingrid Bergman would be Maria, the guerrilla with whom Jordan falls in love.

In the later 1940s and 50s, the novel's critical standing declined compared with some of Hemingway's other works. Readers noted inaccuracies in the use of Spanish in *For Whom the Bell Tolls.* They criticized details of the presentation of Spanish culture, such as the scene where Agustín, a Spanish guerrilla, asks Jordan about Maria's sexual performance. Such curiosity would violate a strict Spanish code of decorum. Other readers said the relationship between Jordan and Maria lacked credibility.

In more recent times the novel has regained critical stature. Some regard it as Hemingway's finest achievement. And few doubt the personal passion and experience he brought to its writing.

How objective a reporter was Hemingway? Can you read *For Whom the Bell Tolls* as an accurate picture of Spain during the civil war? Opinions vary. His war correspondence itself has received labels that range from "stirring accounts" to "a kind of sub-fiction in which he was the central character."

In *For Whom the Bell Tolls* he was objective enough to point out deficiencies of the Republican side and to write vividly of the atrocities they committed. He could also show the enemy in a favorable light. For instance, in the novel's final scene, the representative of the Nationalists, Lieutenant Berrendo, is not an odious barbarian but a richly human character for whom you may feel considerable sympathy.

The famous British writer George Orwell, whose

books include *1984* and *Animal Farm,* was another of the many leading writers who became actively involved in the Spanish Civil War. He wrote *Homage to Catalonia* (1938), a detailed recollection of experiences with one of the Loyalist organizations. You might want to compare the fictional details of *For Whom the Bell Tolls* with Orwell's account of the way he saw the war. You will also learn about the war by reading Arthur Koestler's *Spanish Testament* (1937), a vivid account of the writer's imprisonment by Nationalist forces. *Man's Hope* (1938), by the noted French intellectual André Malraux, is considered a masterly depiction of early stages of the war. In addition, several historical works on the Spanish Civil War contain a wealth of material. Such studies include books by Gabriel Jackson (1965), Hugh Thomas (1977), and Peter Wyden (1983).

Hemingway's second marriage ended in divorce in 1940, and he married Martha Gellhorn, a writer and foreign correspondent during the Spanish Civil War. *For Whom the Bell Tolls* is dedicated to her.

World War II (1939–45) captivated Hemingway. Both his finances and his reputation were solid, and he needed neither the notoriety nor the money from being a war correspondent. Nevertheless, he took a job as chief of the European bureau of *Collier's* magazine. He accompanied the British Royal Air Force on several bombing raids over occupied France and crossed the English Channel with American troops on D-Day, June 6, 1944. He was in the thick of fighting during the liberation of Paris and the Battle of the Bulge, often seeming as much a soldier as a correspondent, according to one source.

In 1945, at the age of 46, Hemingway divorced Martha Gellhorn and married his last wife, Mary Welsh. The couple lived on a luxurious estate outside Havana, Cuba, until the revolution begun in 1959 by Fidel Castro forced them to leave.

Hemingway's novel *Across the River and Into the Trees* (1950) was eagerly awaited. But when published it was scorned, receiving biting, almost vicious, reviews. Critics accused Hemingway of writing self-parody; another claimed to feel "pity, embarrassment, that so fine and honest a writer can make such a travesty of himself." It became fashionable to consider Hemingway washed up as a writer.

Returning to Africa to re-create some of the adventures of the 1930s, Hemingway was nearly killed in an airplane crash. But he survived, and went on to write *The Old Man and the Sea* in 1952, the last major work published while he was alive. (*A Moveable Feast, Islands in the Stream, By-line: Ernest Hemingway*, and *The Dangerous Summer* were published after his death.) *The Old Man and the Sea* revived Hemingway's flagging career. He received a Pulitzer Prize for the book, and it helped him win the prestigious Nobel Prize for literature in 1954.

In subsequent years the hearty and death-defying Hemingway began to lose his health. Nothing, including visits to the Mayo Clinic in Minnesota, was able to restore him to his previous vigor. His illnesses (including a rare disease that affects the vital organs) were compounded by severe states of depression.

Did he decide that, if he could not live as aggressively and boldly as he once had, he would prefer not to live at all? Whatever the reason, he took his own life at his home in Ketchum, Idaho, on July 2, 1961. He shot himself with a silver-inlaid shotgun, choosing a method used by his father years earlier. He thus duplicated an act that he had denounced as cowardly.

Hemingway the artist left a rich legacy of work that has found a permanent place in American literature. That he is likely to endure can be attributed to many factors, but is perhaps best summed up in his own words, spoken to the Writer's Congress in 1937: "A writer's problem . . . is always how to write truly and having found out what is true to project it in such a way that it becomes part of the experience of the person who reads it." Hemingway wrote truly, and he becomes part of everyone who reads him.

THE NOVEL

The Plot

For Whom the Bell Tolls tells the engrossing tale of Robert Jordan, an American supporter of the Republican cause in the Spanish Civil War (1936–39). Within a short span of some 68 hours, Jordan's involvement with a band of guerrillas—notably a young woman named Maria, with whom he falls in love—forces him to question his own participation in a war that seems unwinnable and to realize that the sacrifice of life for the sake of a political cause may be too high a price to pay.

Jordan is a college teacher on a leave of absence in Spain, and as *For Whom the Bell Tolls* opens, he's discussing the location of a bridge with a local guide named Anselmo. But there's much more to the situation than that. The Spain that Jordan loves is involved in a civil war, and he has really come to help wage that war on behalf of the side he believes in. At the moment his job is to blow up a bridge behind enemy lines.

The assignment came to Jordan through General Golz, a Soviet officer also in Spain to help fight the war. According to Golz, the demolition of the bridge at precisely the right moment is a key part of a large-scale offensive by the Republican forces.

Jordan needs help to do the job, so the peasant Anselmo has brought him to a guerrilla band hiding in the mountains. From the moment Jordan meets Pablo, their leader, Jordan suspects that the guerrilla chief, who should be his chief ally in the operation, will spell trouble.

Pablo has "gone bad." He's lost his drive, his purpose as a guerrilla leader. He's content simply to stay hidden and survive, rather than actively harass the enemy.

With the arrival of Jordan, the band of seven men and two women are given a renewed sense of purpose. This prompts a showdown for leadership of the band. Pilar, Pablo's mistress, publicly assumes charge. Pablo's status is uncertain at this moment, and several of the band would now be grateful if Jordan killed Pablo. But he doesn't. Plans are made to enlist the help of a neighboring guerrilla band, led by El Sordo, in the demolition of the bridge.

Robert Jordan finds more than the bridge to occupy his attention. Among the guerrilla group is Maria, a young woman who was rescued by the band during their last significant operation. They are almost instantly attracted to each other and spend this first night making love. It's not the first sexual experience for either of them. Jordan has been with other women; Maria was once raped by a group of enemy soldiers. But for each, it's the first experience that combines sex with love.

On the second day, Jordan, Pilar, and Maria make their way to the hideout of El Sordo to enlist his help in demolishing the bridge. El Sordo promises support. On the return trip, Pilar deliberately leaves Jordan and Maria by themselves for a while. Again they make love, and Jordan begins to entertain serious doubts about whether this war is the most important thing in his life after all.

The band now observes a heavy concentration of enemy soldiers riding through the area but manages to avoid detection. El Sordo and his men are not so fortunate. Nationalist soldiers—the enemy—trap them on a hill and they are slaughtered. Jordan and the others hear the sounds of the fighting but are helpless to come to El Sordo's aid. It's an agonizing feeling.

Personal experiences have brought Jordan to doubt the value of this war in general. Now the concentration of enemy soldiers and planes in the area makes him doubt the practicality of blowing up the bridge. Perhaps if Golz were aware of the enemy's numbers in the immediate area, he would want the operation canceled.

He writes a dispatch to Golz. But the messenger is delayed time and again—not by the presence of the enemy in the area, but by the frustrating bumbling and petty bureaucracy of his own Republican forces. Ultimately, he is arrested and the dispatch is confiscated, again by his own people.

At the camp, Maria and Jordan dream about their future together, but Jordan knows they are fooling themselves. Finally, Pilar brings Jordan the news that Pablo has deserted and has taken the detonation devices. The bridge operation wasn't easy to begin with; now Jordan will have to improvise a makeshift exploder and detonators just to have a chance at succeeding.

He spends the middle of the night devising a way—and holding Maria. "We'll be killed but we'll blow the bridge," he whispers to her as she sleeps in his arms.

Early on the morning of this fourth day, as the band eat what could be their last breakfast, Pablo returns. He apologizes for his moment of weakness. To make up for it, he has brought several more men from the area to join them. But the exploder and detonators are gone; he has tossed them in the river.

Meanwhile, a Soviet journalist secures the release of the messenger, and Jordan's dispatch finally reaches Golz, but it's too late. The doomed attack has already been mounted and can't be stopped.

Without counterorders from Golz, Jordan's mission to blow up the bridge proceeds. He feverishly rigs the improvised detonation devices just in time. At the sound of the Loyalist attack (his cue), the bridge is blown up. Jordan has accomplished what he came to do. But he is a different man from what he was a short while ago; the success gives him little satisfaction.

The band must now attempt a retreat. Pablo, the most familiar with the area, has devised a workable plan. The group draws enemy fire but no one is hit. They all have a chance to escape to a safe area—except Robert Jordan.

His horse is hit and falls on him, breaking his thigh. For the good of all, he is left behind. Everyone but Maria can see that there is no other way. There is a painful good-bye. Maria protests to the end and won't leave until she is forced to by Pilar and Pablo.

Robert Jordan struggles to remain conscious just

long enough to kill at least some of the enemy. He lies on the ground, awaiting the enemy.

The Characters
MAJOR CHARACTERS

Robert Jordan

Robert Jordan is a man of action. In *For Whom the Bell Tolls*, he undertakes a dangerous mission, even welcomes it. Like other Hemingway heroes, he seems to understand that dying well can be even more important than living well.

But unlike other Hemingway heroes, Jordan believes in an abstract ideal, an ideology, a cause. This cause is "government by the people" in the Spain that he loves. Jordan's liberal political views have motivated him to leave the University of Montana where he teaches Spanish, in order to fight with the Spanish Republicans, or Loyalists. Whereas most liberal intellectuals were willing only to denounce in words the rise of fascism in Spain, Jordan takes action in support of his political beliefs.

Beyond that, Jordan is intelligent, clever, inventive, and decisive. He can keep his composure in sticky situations. These qualities are necessary for survival in his role in Spain of a demolition expert behind enemy lines.

Jordan is unquestionably in charge, except in the arena of his own mind. Here, he begins to question and reevaluate the very ideals that brought him to Spain. This tormented individualist sways and wavers, experiencing moments of painful honesty and moments of self-deception. He sometimes feels caught between new values emerging in his life and a duty he has committed himself to.

At the conclusion of Hemingway's story, dedication to an ideology is not as important to Jordan as it was at the beginning. He begins to see that his cause is tarnished, that perhaps every cause is tarnished. He has changed from a believer in abstract ideas to a believer in the importance of the individual person.

You might accept this change as both credible and authentic, or you might question it on the grounds that it's motivated principally by his rather swift and passionate love affair with Maria. You'll have to decide whether Jordan is more genuine or less genuine at the conclusion of the novel—or equally so, even though his principal allegiance has changed.

Pablo

Pablo, the leader of the guerrilla band, is one of Hemingway's richest characters. In one sense he is quite entertaining, not only because he is frequently comically drunk but also because his behavior is full of surprises.

At one time, there had been an entirely different Pablo, who, like Jordan, believed strongly in the Loyalist cause. But unlike Jordan, that Pablo was capable of immense cruelty.

Now the guerrilla leader is disillusioned. The cause means little to him. He's content simply to survive, hidden in the mountains, doing almost nothing to aid the Loyalist forces. Given his horses and his wine, he appears happy.

On the surface, he seems to have degenerated into an ineffective force. But he cannot be discounted. In fact, his bitter disillusionment makes him dangerous. He's capable now of deliberately sabotaging the very operations he formerly supported and led.

Yet something of the old Pablo remains. He may have lost his motivation and the firmness of his allegiance, but he hasn't lost his cleverness and expertise as a guerrilla soldier.

During the course of the story, Pablo doesn't actually change, as Robert Jordan does. He vacillates. He is now one Pablo, now another—a frustrating figure to Jordan, and probably to you, also.

But most of the time Pablo suffers from what we might call burnout, exhaustion and apathy resulting usually from working too hard at something. What's responsible for this disintegration of Pablo from a terror-wielding firebrand to an often drunken excuse for a soldier?

Several possibilities exist. One is his dependence on wine. You may see that as a defect of character or as a disease. Or it could be that the responsibility of leading his band during wartime has simply worn him down. Perhaps through lack of willpower he has allowed fear to transform him into a spineless character. Maybe he has simply become soft and spoiled by the relative luxuries of his recently sheltered situation.

A particularly intriguing line of thought is that Pablo suffers from guilt over the atrocities he engineered at the beginning of the war, which Pilar describes in Chapter 10. Guilt can produce severe depression leading to inactivity and even virtual paralysis. At one point Pablo does express a sor-

row for having killed and a kinship with his victims, but it's uncertain whether this is Pablo or his
red wine speaking.

Pilar

Pilar is Pablo's mistress and the real leader of the
guerrilla band, even though Pablo nominally holds
the title at the beginning of the novel. As with
Pablo, there is more than one Pilar. But she is far
more predictable. In fact, you typically see only
her tough side. Whatever the situation, Pilar is always in charge.

She is duly respectful of Jordan's status with the
movement and his expertise as a demolition expert. But she is prepared to set him straight when
she feels it's needed.

She is a woman born into a male-oriented culture. Thus she is domestic in many ways. She even
trains Maria in some traditional household and man-
pleasing "duties." At the same time, she can carry
heavy equipment, fire a machine gun, and command a group of seasoned, male guerrilla soldiers.

She is rough and hardened, capable of crude
speech and outrageous insults. She dispenses them
freely, particularly to Pablo. Anyone who strikes
her as acting stupidly is a target for her acid tongue.

Though physically ugly—by her own admission—Pilar has not lacked for lovers. She recalls
her former lover Finito with a nostalgic fondness.
She is affectionate with Maria, for whom she has
genuine feelings. And her strength diminishes at
times—the roar of plane engines overhead sends
her into a shudder of fear.

True to her complex character, when Pablo returns from his brief desertion, she insults, forgives, then admires him nearly all in the same breath.

Unlike Pablo, throughout most of the story Pilar professes to be a fervent believer in the Republican movement as an ideal. In that respect she is like the Robert Jordan we see at the beginning of the story. You might question how genuine this is or at least what motivates Pilar. You might see her as truly convinced of Republican ideals, even though she could not articulate them in the intellectual manner that Jordan would. Another interpretation is that she has simply found her niche in this turbulent wartime situation and receives sufficient psychological reward to keep her going from her role as behind-the-scenes controller of what is nominally Pablo's band. It might even be argued that both the above compensate for her recent lack of romantic and sexual fulfillment with Pablo.

There is also a mystical streak in Pilar. Although full of common sense, she is attuned to mysteries of the universe. She reads Jordan's palm and probably sees his imminent death. She also graphically recounts the smell of death that clung to the ill-fated Kashkin, Jordan's predecessor.

Maria

Maria is a young Spanish woman who was rescued by Pablo's band when they hijacked a Nationalist train. She has been with them since. Maria is important in the story as a principal cause of character development in Robert Jordan. But many readers feel that she herself changes little and is a superficial character. One commentator has said that even Jordan's fantasies of love affairs with screen goddesses are more real than the portrait of Maria.

At their first meeting, she is strongly attracted to Jordan. She exhibits an almost desperate need for the attentions of a man who will care for her as a woman—but with respect and tenderness.

Crucial to this need is a nightmare of Maria's past: the brutal rape she experienced at the hands of her Nationalist captors. Pilar has afforded some healing with her philosophy that whatever Maria didn't actually consent to did not, in a sense, happen—or at least did not count. But Maria needs more than this.

You might question whether Maria's willingness to give herself so quickly and completely to Jordan is believable in light of her previous brutal treatment at the hands of men. After all, even though Jordan fights for the Loyalists, as a person he's an unknown quantity to her.

Finding Jordan both masculine and gentle, Maria becomes lovingly subservient to a degree that some women readers find somewhat silly. She talks almost in terms of worship. As you read the novel, you'll have to decide whether Hemingway has portrayed Maria's relationship with Jordan in believable terms.

At the close of the story, Maria and Jordan's relationship is, in their own words, much deeper than simple attraction and need. Has Maria herself changed—or been changed? Or has something good (a sincere love affair) simply happened to her while she herself remains much the same person?

SELECTED MINOR CHARACTERS

Anselmo

Anselmo, the oldest member of the guerrilla band, never uses his age as an excuse for shirking work for the Republican cause. There is nothing half-hearted about his service. Above all, he exhibits simplicity and integrity. Many readers feel that when Anselmo speaks, it's worth listening to.

Anselmo is also a gentle, sensitive man who is able to see enemy soldiers as men very much like himself. The killing involved in the guerrilla band's operations causes him much pain. At heart he is a deeply religious man.

Thus, even in a situation he did not devise or wish for, Anselmo seems to be an example of an honest gentleman. His integrity combined with the nominal atheism he must subscribe to on behalf of the Republicans have gained him the epithet "secular saint" in some critiques.

Yet it's possible to see him in another light. Given the depth of his religious and ethical convictions, which become particularly evident at the end of the novel, why hasn't he simply stood up and said "I will not serve" a cause which exercises the killing and brutality which he hates?

General Golz

Golz is a Soviet military strategist who is in Spain to help the Republican forces. But it's difficult to determine his personal involvement in the cause. He devotes himself to his job, and he's upset (as Jordan will be) at the incompetent manner in which the Loyalists wage the war. He is resentful that amateurish bumbling and pettiness prevent his strategic plans from being carried out as he has ordered.

This could be explained by a sincere belief in his communist ideology and a desire to see justice and self-determination granted to the common people of Spain. It could also stem from a love of playing professional war games and a desire for a sparkling military record. Golz, after all, will not answer to the people of Spain. He answers to superiors who will determine his career as a Soviet officer.

El Sordo

El Sordo ("The Deaf One") is the leader of a neighboring guerrilla band. He's an aggressive leader such as Pablo once was, although perhaps without the cruelty. He's courageous, resourceful, and dedicated to the Republic.

But he's also a realist: he has no illusions about the possibility of Republican success in the civil war. In this respect, he can be seen as the purest example of devotion to an ideal. He knows that the cause for which he will die will fail. Yet he does more than he has to on its behalf. He even gives Jordan (who is expected to return to the luxury of the United States) a rare bottle of whiskey in hospitable thanks for Jordan's aid toward the cause.

He can also be seen as a contradictory character. Although he does not accept the collectivist slogans that promise victory or at least glory through sustained effort, he fights with all his effort on behalf of the force which generates them.

Karkov

Karkov is a Soviet journalist covering the Spanish Civil War from his headquarters in Madrid. He seems to give allegiance to the ideology of the Republic. Consequently, the bumbling and indifference that he observes in many of its higher echelons disgust and infuriate him.

He's similar to Golz in that it's difficult to determine how personally he's involved in the cause. While on the surface he seems genuine, he doesn't hesitate to avail himself of the relatively extravagant luxuries at Gaylord's Hotel, the Soviet headquarters in Madrid. In this manner, he could easily symbolize many who have thrown themselves into the cause of the common, impoverished people— but without truly wanting to share their general lot in life.

Joaquín

Joaquín is a young, idealistic member of El Sordo's band. At the time of the air attack on the guerrillas, Joaquín at first is a vocal partisan of the communist cause. But as the attack begins and the possibility of death looms, Joaquín returns to his Roman Catholic roots and begins to pray fervently.

Andrés

Andrés is a member of Pablo's band. He is sent by Jordan to deliver the message to General Golz that the planned Republican offensive has been anticipated by the enemy.

Other Elements
SETTING

Because *For Whom the Bell Tolls* is set during the Spanish Civil War, it is important to know some of the elements of Spanish geography incorporated in the book. If you look at the series of maps entitled "The Course of the Spanish Civil War" (page 25), you'll notice the increase of Nationalist-held territory from July 1936 to October 1937. (The novel takes place in May 1937.) By 1937 the Republicans were steadily losing ground, and Robert Jordan's mission—to blow up a bridge crucial to enemy Nationalist interests—takes on added importance.

Almost in the center of Spain is Madrid, the capital, once a Republican stronghold, but in May 1937 close to falling to the enemy. To the north of Madrid (see map on page 28) is the Guadarrama Range, where Pablo's band is hiding and where the bridge is to be demolished. The town of La Granja is where members of the band go for supplies and news of the war. To the southwest of the Guadarrama mountains is the Gredos Range, where Pablo intends to retreat after the bridge is blown up. To the west of the Guadarrama Range is the city of Segovia, a Nationalist stronghold the Republicans hope to capture in their offensive.

Farther northwest of Segovia is Valladolid, where Maria was taken prisoner. It was there she was transported by the train that Pablo's band seized and blew up.

Notice, too, the region of Estremadura in the western part of Spain, where Jordan was working before his current assignment.

Many readers have pointed out that one of Ernest Hemingway's major goals in writing *For Whom the Bell Tolls* was to demonstrate that the real victims of the Spanish Civil War were the Spanish people themselves, torn by the savage self-interest of the competing political ideologues. The tragic

The Course of the Spanish Civil War

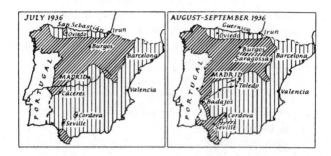

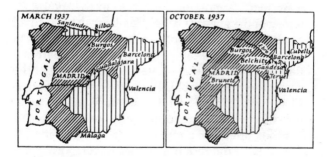

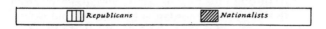

effects of a brutal war on the peasants for whom it had become a daily reality are revealed in the rebel camp where Jordan and the others are hiding. These simple, earthy people have been transformed permanently by the war, and its toll is immeasurable. Hemingway shows us the cost of war in a variety of ways: Pilar's lengthy and vivid description of the atrocities inflicted upon Nationalist enemies in her village; Maria's suffering at the hands of the enemy; Pablo's erratic behavior; Anselmo's pathetic conflict between loyalty to the cause and his dislike of killing, to name the most obvious examples. Because the fate of the Spanish people (mostly farmers) is so directly tied to the land the war has ravaged, they act as an indivisible part of the novel's setting.

By placing most of the action in the mountain retreat of the guerrilla band, Hemingway has created a setting that is symbolic in contrasting ways. On the one hand, the camp hidden in the Guadarrama Range is a refuge that offers safety for many of the characters. Here Pablo, Pilar, and the other guerrillas have come to find temporary safety; here, too, Maria has come to heal physical and psychic wounds after her imprisonment by the Nationalists. It is in the mountains that Robert Jordan begins to question his motives as a participant in this war: through his love for Maria and his association with the peasants, Jordan is humanized and slowly comes to realize the truth of the quotation from John Donne at the opening of the novel: "No man is an Iland."

On the other hand, the mountain hideout also represents the plight of the Republicans—there they are trapped, blocked by fascist troops below them and enemy aircraft whizzing over their heads. The snow of the mountains offers a similar two-sided symbol: beautiful to look at, it suggests nature at its most peaceful, but the snow is also deadly, since it reveals the whereabouts of the rebels once they have walked in it.

HISTORICAL BACKGROUND

Until the 1930s Spain had been a monarchy for centuries, except for a brief experiment as a republic in 1873–74. We can begin the background to the Spanish Civil War with Alfonso XIII, who came to the Spanish throne in 1902. The general verdict of historians is that he was incompetent. In 1921, for example, 20,000 Spanish troops died in an ill-conceived, unsuccessful offensive that he ordered against Moroccan tribes. He subsequently disbanded Parliament and selected Miguel Primo de Rivera as a military dictator.

Rivera established a dictatorship with Alfonso as figurehead. Although Rivera's government, which held power from 1923 to 1930, initially proved efficient and was widely favored, its popularity later declined and finally even the army withdrew its support. Rivera fled in January 1930, leaving Alfonso with the huge problem of trying to run Spain with little popular support.

In the hope of avoiding civil war, Alfonso went into exile, attempting to do so with a touch of grace by not officially abdicating. In 1931 the Second Republic, led by a coalition of Socialists and middle-class liberals, was formed amid enthusiasm.

But the new government tried to do too much too quickly—and often acted unwisely. This was

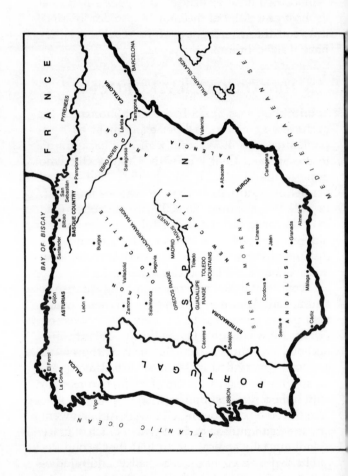

especially the case in matters of educational reform and in trying to reduce the immense power of both the church and the army.

Consequently, opposition mounted. Monarchist plots arose on behalf of Alfonso and even on behalf of the line of Don Carlos, the 19th-century claimant to the throne. By the end of 1935, twenty-eight governments had been formed and had fallen. The country was close to chaos, with frequent strikes and uprisings by self-declared autonomous governments.

The election of February 1936 gave power to the Popular Front, a shaky mixture of Republicans, Socialists, Communists, and Anarchists. But wide-scale disorder and violence continued to rack the country. Spain had finally gained a government "of the people," but the Republic was weak and inefficient—and thus its own worst enemy.

The situation begged for a force to bring order out of chaos and hence was ripe for the formation and growth of fascist organizations based on the premise of a strong central government. Principal among the fascist groups was the Falange, begun by José Antonio Primo de Rivera, the son of the previous dictator, Miguel Primo de Rivera.

Many tradition-minded Spanish people, particularly the landowners and conservative army officers, began to feel that their way of life would be destroyed either by official government reforms or by the general chaos of the country. They started planning to overthrow the government.

The army made its move on July 17, 1936, charging that the government could not keep order. It was certainly not the first fighting in Spain. But it was the beginning of large-scale civil war, with the lines clearly drawn.

The forces led by the army (with General Francisco Franco in charge) were called the Nationalists or Rebels. Supporting the Nationalists were monarchists, Carlists (monarchists who supported the claim of descendants of Don Carlos, rather than the Bourbon line), the wealthy upper classes, the Falange fascists, and elements of the Roman Catholic Church.

The forces defending the Republican government were called Loyalists or Republicans. This group included much of the working class and most liberals, socialists, and communists.

The Spanish Civil War was a brutal conflict that included many appalling acts of cruelty and terrorism. The Nationalist forces often found themselves in the position of an alien invading army. Popular sympathy was usually with the Republicans, but the support was largely passive. One way the Nationalists tried to gain control of people was through terror: torture, executions, and bloodletting of all kinds. Loyalists responded with equally reprehensible atrocities, like those described in Chapter 10 of *For Whom the Bell Tolls*.

The Spanish Civil War was, in part, an international affair. Historians have often commented that the war served as a training ground, almost a dress rehearsal, for World War II.

Aiding the Nationalists were approximately 50,000 soldiers from Fascist Italy, 20,000 from Portugal, and 10,000 from Nazi Germany. These countries also provided modern war materials.

On the Republican side were Soviet soldiers, well trained and able to assume positions of leadership, and an estimated 40,000 additional volunteers from around the globe, including the United States. The volunteers were mostly professional soldiers for hire, international adventurers, or persons who sympathized ideologically with the Republicans. This last group included people like Robert Jordan, the main character in *For Whom the Bell Tolls.*

Some arms and equipment were sent to the Loyalists from such countries as the Soviet Union, Mexico, and France, but this aid didn't equal that provided to the Nationalists. Consequently, Nationalist forces were nearly always better equipped.

The Nationalist rebels began by occupying the northwest and the southern tip of Spain and gradually linked these two areas. From there they executed a pincer movement: down from the north, up from the south, and toward the Mediterranean coast in the east.

By the spring of 1937, when *For Whom the Bell Tolls* takes place, the Nationalists were making serious inroads in Republican-controlled territory. Madrid, the Spanish capital, was held by the Republicans but was constantly under siege. The guerrilla camp depicted by Hemingway in the novel was behind Nationalist lines, about sixty miles from Madrid. It was also during this time, on April 26, that Nazi German airplanes bombed the Basque town of Guernica, killing more than 1600 civilians. Guernica was without military importance, and the bombing brought an international outcry of protest. The incident also inspired one of Spanish painter Pablo Picasso's most vivid and moving paintings, called *Guernica,* created out of his heartbreak and rage.

Yet for all the Nationalist gains in 1937, the Republicans remained hopeful they could win the war. Hemingway has called this period of brave optimism "the happiest period of our lives," referring to those sympathizers and journalists who were in Spain. But less than two years later, in March 1939, Madrid was captured by the Nationalists, and the war was over.

The toll in human lives was immense. Nearly 110,000 people died in battles and air raids. Some 220,000 persons were murdered or executed. About 200,000 Loyalist prisoners were shot or died of ill-treatment in prison cells even after the Nationalist triumph. And more than 300,000 people sought exile abroad.

THEMES

The following are themes of *For Whom the Bell Tolls*.

Major Themes

1. RELATIONSHIP OF THE INDIVIDUAL TO MANKIND

Hemingway's choice of a John Donne poem as the source of the novel's title and epigraph emphasizes a major theme of *For Whom the Bell Tolls:* "No man is an iland," that is, no person can exist separate from the lives of others, even others living in far-away countries.

The theme is demonstrated most clearly by the actions of Robert Jordan. Throughout his participation in the Spanish Civil War, he has fought actively for a cause—not the cause of communism, as he says, but the cause of antifascism. As the novel progresses, his involvement with the guerrilla band, and particularly his love for Maria, teach

him the value of the individual as he or she affects
a larger society. The abstractions of an ideology
are lifeless without the people they represent; con-
cepts have no meaning except for the ways in which
they affect human beings.

For Jordan, Maria represents human love, the
first he has ever known. It is for her that he stays
behind to allow the rest of the band to escape,
demonstrating his realization that others depend
on him as he has depended on them. His decision
not to commit suicide at the end of the novel represents his ultimate understanding that he must
fight for the people whose lives are affected by the
cause, not purely for the cause as a generalized
ideology.

Both Pablo and Pilar represent minor variations
of the theme of interdependency. Pablo is full of
greedy self-interest now that he owns horses. His
decision to betray the guerrilla band is due to his
need to survive and thrive. At the last minute,
however, he seems to understand how his actions
will affect those whom he once led, and he returns
to help them. Pilar, on the other hand, is almost
blindly devoted to the cause. She will do whatever
it takes to win for the Republic. Yet she, too, comes
to understand the severe toll the guerrillas' mission is likely to take, and for the first time she
expresses doubt about the cause that prompted the
demolition.

2. NATURE OF THE SPANISH CIVIL WAR
Who wants the Spanish Civil War? Is anyone
likely to benefit from it? Look for answers to these
questions as you read *For Whom the Bell Tolls*. There
is much to suggest that the common people, on

whose behalf the war is supposedly being waged, are tired of the war, uninterested in it, and unlikely to benefit from it. Readers have pointed out that Hemingway was prompted in part to write *For Whom the Bell Tolls* to show his disgust at the way in which the civil war had betrayed the Spanish people, both through internal disputes between the warring factions and through foreign intervention eager for a testing ground for an upcoming war.

The war's effect on the Spanish is demonstrated in acts of great courage and great cruelty. The challenges of the struggle created both the bloodthirstiness and greed of Pablo, as well as the steadfast courage of Pilar and Anselmo. The war may have exacted a terrible price from its people, Hemingway seems to be saying, but it often revealed them at their best.

Despite his pro-Republican leanings, Hemingway is careful to point out that both sides are capable of savage behavior and that each side is peopled with human beings with similar human needs. Through Robert Jordan, Hemingway describes how a foreigner comes to view the Spanish struggle. Jordan often states his belief in the "power, justice, and equality to the people" theory espoused by the Republicans. But he soon sees the toll the war is taking on those around him, and he realizes, too, that his own side has commited as many outrages against human rights as the enemy has.

3. LOVE
Hemingway writes about several kinds of love in *For Whom the Bell Tolls*. Romantic love is depicted in the relationship of Jordan and Maria. Be-

fore Maria, Jordan had expressed himself sexually, but he had not loved. Loving her transports him from his intellectual world of ideology to the world of real-life relationships. Maria represents the love that humanizes Jordan, making possible his transition from a political partisan to one who recognizes the worth of the individual. For Maria, Jordan's love is the healing touch she needs to cure the psychic wounds inflicted upon her by her former captors.

Other kinds of love also are discussed in the novel. Many of the peasants in the guerrilla band demonstrate a fierce love of the land that supports their involvement in this brutal war. Jordan's love of liberty has brought him to Spain to fight for the Republican cause. The anguish of Pablo's band as the guerrillas listen to the attack on El Sordo's camp reflects the love among comrades. And Pilar's concern for Maria's happiness and well-being is a kind of maternal love that plays a part in Maria's healing process.

4. DEATH

In Hemingway's novels, heroes are often involved in activities that risk death—in fact, they might be said to court death. Robert Jordan is no exception, and from the beginning of *For Whom the Bell Tolls* death is a palpable presence. Jordan's job as demolition expert is filled with danger, and there are numerous foreshadowings of his fate, such as the death of Kashkin, his predeccessor, and the troubling information Pilar reads in his palm (but won't divulge).

Death also is linked to the novel's major theme of interdependency. The deaths that occur during the story as well as Kashkin's, which occurs before the novel opens, affect the lives of others. Kashkin's death, for example, affects Jordan and the members of the guerrilla band. El Sordo's death has serious consequences for the members of the camp. Jordan is haunted by the deaths of his father and grandfather. And Jordan's decision to hold off his own death by not committing suicide is made in order to save the lives of the others who are trying to flee the enemy. Just as one man's life can have a strong effect on those around him, so his death can have similar consequences.

5. HYPOCRISY

Examples of hypocrisy abound in *For Whom the Bell Tolls*. Prime among them are the Loyalist leaders themselves, many of whom are incompetent and uncaring. They exploit their positions in order to attain a level of comfort and self-indulgence in the midst of war.

Many of the leaders who were supposed to have sprung directly from the Spanish peasantry at the beginning of the war are not really genuine, and in fact some have been imported.

In his musings, Jordan admits that he doesn't really believe all the things he says he believes in order to justify his involvement in the war.

The communist slogans that Joaquín mouths as El Sordo's band is being besieged provide further examples of a philosophy that does not seem to work, yet is regarded by many as sacred.

The crowning touch is André Marty, the visiting French communist leader. Although many regard him with awe, his incompetence regularly sends men to their death—while career officers stand around and do nothing about it. He embodies both tactical bungling and self-centered hypocrisy.

Minor Themes
1. FATE AND MYSTICISM
From the beginning of the story, when Pilar "reads" Robert Jordan's hand, there are hints at an unseen, unavoidable force in control of events. It would be easy for Jordan to dismiss what Pilar sees as mere superstition. But he doesn't, even though he claims not to believe in such things; what she may have seen of his future concerns him a great deal.

2. THE CODE HERO
Hemingway did not coin the term code hero. It evolved from the attempts of critics to describe the type of protagonist Hemingway frequently placed in his novels.

"Code" here means a set of rules or guidelines for conduct. The principal ideals in the code are honor, courage, and stoic endurance through stress, misfortune, and pain. The hero's world is often violent and disorderly; moreover, the violence and disorder seem to prevail.

The code dictates that the hero act honorably even in the midst of what will be a losing battle. In doing so, he finds fulfillment. He achieves or proves his manhood and his worth. The term "grace under pressure" is often used to describe the conduct of the Hemingway code hero.

Robert Jordan fits this mold in many ways, although he is more introspective, more thoughtful, and less physical than other Hemingway heroes (such as Jake Barnes in *The Sun Also Rises* and Harry Morgan in *To Have and Have Not*).

3. RELIGION

On the surface, religion does not come across favorably in the pages of *For Whom the Bell Tolls*. Characters like Lieutenant Berrendo order atrocities and utter prayers almost in the same breath. One character, Joaquín, reveals the conflict that many of the characters underwent as their own religious beliefs were forcibly replaced with communist theories. He returns to his Roman Catholic prayers just as he thinks death is near.

Some readers feel that Hemingway is criticizing religion as an emotional "band-aid." But others say that his portrayal of religion suggests that a relationship with God is built into the human condition, and that neither evil nor official atheism can eradicate it.

STYLE

Rarely have authors become so identified with a particular writing style or with the word "style" itself as Ernest Hemingway. Many writers have attempted to "write like Hemingway." Few have succeeded.

To many readers, the essential characteristic of the Hemingway style is simplicity and precision of word choice. That description, while accurate, can be deceptive.

"Simplicity" is not the same thing as short, grammatically simple sentences. "Precision of word choice" does not mean an abundance of unusual words in order to achieve precision. And Hemingway's style cannot so easily be explained as in his own often quoted advice (which needs to be taken with a grain of salt!) to write the story and then remove the adjectives and adverbs.

At the conclusion of *For Whom the Bell Tolls*, you will have a distinct picture of the places, the objects, the people in the story. If you diagrammed or sketched them, they might be somewhat different from another reader's mental picture. That's inevitable. It's the distinctness—giving the reader the feeling of being there—which is Hemingway's literary feat.

Beyond question this effect is achieved by a heavy use of nouns and verbs. If there is an object in the scene he is relating, Hemingway will mention it. If a character moves, Hemingway will mention it.

It is true that Hemingway often leaves the adjectives and adverbs to the reader. The resulting effect is all the more vivid and memorable. An excellent example is the description of the sights and smells both inside and outside the cave, at the opening of Chapter 5. At the same time, Hemingway does not avoid modifiers altogether. A good example is the description of Joaquín when he is first introduced at the beginning of Chapter 11.

Much has been made of Hemingway's dialogue, through which you get the feeling of being at the scene. Yet when the dialogue is transferred to the motion picture screen, directors have had to be careful to keep it from sounding stilted and formal, because its effectiveness does not depend on reproducing the exact words (including the "uh's" and "er's") that people utter in real life. Hemingway also doesn't often punctuate his dialogue with italics, capital letters, ellipses (. . .), and exclamation points to suggest emphasis. The effectiveness lies in stating with utmost simplicity the heart of what the characters mean.

In general, however, *For Whom the Bell Tolls* is often regarded as somewhat of a stylistic departure from Hemingway's earlier novels, such as *The Sun Also Rises*. Earlier works relied more heavily on colloquial dialogue to communicate action and rarely included lengthy descriptive passages. Some experts have suggested that in *For Whom the Bell Tolls*, Hemingway was responding to criticisms of his style. In this, his longest novel, he inserted lengthy lyric passages that describe the countryside, portrayed the mind of Robert Jordan with extended interior monologues, and replaced flowing conversation with a sometimes stilted attempt to reproduce the Spanish language. The leanness of the prose in his earlier novels—which prompted critics to call him a major literary innovator—was thus sacrificed for what some consider pretentiousness, but what others see as brave and successful strides in experimentation. Those who disliked his work in *For Whom the Bell Tolls* were pleased when he returned to a simpler, terser style in works like *The Old Man and the Sea*.

* * *

Stylistic features peculiar to *For Whom the Bell Tolls* should be noted. They concern Hemingway's deliberate attempt to reproduce in English the flavor of the Spanish language.

Spanish (like other languages) preserves a special second-person singular pronoun and related verb form, such as English formerly had (thou, thy, thee). This form is used in speaking to another person in a familiar manner. Hemingway uses the antiquated English form to better approximate the speech of his Spanish characters. Readers differ in their reactions to this device. Some find it awkward and distracting. Others find that it begins to sound natural after a while. You'll recognize other English sentences that display strange word order or style, such as "That this thing of the bridge may succeed." This kind of construction is also an attempt to capture the flavor of the Spanish language.

Both Hemingway's actual Spanish and his attempt to render the flavor of Spanish in English have been criticized as frequently inaccurate by people who know Spanish better than he did. An exiled Loyalist commander, Gustavo Duran, read the manuscript of *For Whom the Bell Tolls* before it was published and was critical of Hemingway's Spanish, although impressed by the story. A more contemporary Spanish critic has called the language abstract when it should be concrete (to properly mirror real Spanish) and solemn when it should be simple.

Hemingway also tries to convey the extremely physical and earthy—often crude—dialogue of Spanish peasants (particularly when they are upset with each other). Today, when there is very little censorship in the publishing industry, there would be no problem in printing the exact English equivalent of what Hemingway wanted his Spanish characters to say. But in 1940 there was a problem in using obscenities.

One of Hemingway's solutions was simply to quote the original Spanish word or phrase. It's then up to the reader to check with a Spanish/English dictionary to learn how crudely someone has insulted someone else.

A second method was to employ an all-purpose and acceptable English word that at least suggests the original. Anselmo, in his early tirade about Pablo's negative attitude, says: "I this and that in the this and that of thy father. I this and that and that in thy this." On several occasions one character advises another to "Go unprint thyself."

POINT OF VIEW

There are many ways for a writer to tell a story. Point of view depends in part on the author's decision concerning *who* tells the story. Is it someone intimately involved with the action of the story? Someone who was merely a minor participant? Someone who has an omniscient view of everything and can see into the minds of one or all of the characters?

Hemingway considered the first-person point-of-view (in which one of the story's characters narrates the action) effective but limited. He said that it took him a while to master the third-person omniscient point-of-view used in *For Whom the Bell Tolls*, in which the narrator knows everything and reports the inner thoughts and feelings of the characters.

Most of the time, Robert Jordan is at the center of the scene, and it is his thoughts that we listen in on. But there are exceptions. Chapter 15, for example, spotlights Anselmo and his soul searching. In Chapter 27, El Sordo reveals the thoughts that occupy his last hours. These occasional departures from Jordan's consciousness serve to create a fuller, more rounded picture of the world the novel portrays.

FORM AND STRUCTURE

For Whom the Bell Tolls is a finely crafted novel that builds to a powerful climax. The novel covers approximately sixty-eight hours, outlined as follows:

first day	late afternoon to midnight	6 to 8 hours
second day	complete	24 hours
third day	complete	24 hours
fourth day	midnight to afternoon	15 to 17 hours

The technique of flashback is used sparingly but effectively. The most notable example is in Chapter 10, where Pilar describes the brutality that Pablo inflicted on the leading men of a Nationalist town his band had taken. Strictly speaking, this is indirect flashback, since it comes through Pilar's narration, rather than through a directly presented scene.

Other significant flashbacks include Jordan's painful recollection in Chapter 30 of his father's suicide and Maria's moving account in Chapter 31 of her abuse at the hands of Nationalist soldiers.

Hemingway heightens the suspense in the final chapters (33 to 43) by devoting alternating chapters to two strands of the story line. The odd-numbered chapters are devoted to Jordan at the scene of the demolition. The even-numbered chapters (with the exception of 38) feature Andrés on his mission to find Golz and deliver Jordan's dispatch.

The bridge, described masterfully as "solid flung metal grace" forms the center of the novel. Few readers find the bridge itself to be symbolic, but the entire action of the novel radiates from it—it is the reason Jordan has come to the guerrilla camp, it is important to both sides at this point in the war, and the decision to blow it up is a matter of intense controversy among the Republicans hiding in the mountains. Virtually every movement in the novel is directed toward or away from the bridge and is occasioned by the plan to blow it up.

The Story

No man is an *Iland*, intire of it selfe; every man is a peece of the *Continent*, a part of the *maine*; if a *Clod* bee washed away by the *Sea, Europe* is the lesse, as well as if a *Promontorie* were, as well as if a *Mannor* of thy *friends* or of *thine owne* were; any mans *death* diminishes *me*, because I am involved in *Mankinde*; And therefore never send to know for whom the *bell* tolls; It tolls for *thee*.

—John Donne

Hemingway used this excerpt from the English poet John Donne (1572–1631) as an epigraph to *For Whom the Bell Tolls*. Its significance will become more apparent as you accompany Robert Jordan through the next few days of his life.

CHAPTER 1

It's a peaceful scene: a young man is lying on a pine-needled forest floor. A gently flowing stream and a mill complete the placid, country picture. An old man answers the young man's questions about the countryside.

Think of a time when you were in a situation where the *appearances* of the surroundings contrasted with what was really going on. Perhaps something very serious was happening in your life on a bright, apparently carefree day.

That seems to be the situation here. Hemingway first hints at the seriousness of the scene by mentioning the young man's military map. You can be sure this is no pleasure trip when Anselmo, an old Spanish peasant who is Robert Jordan's guide behind enemy lines, asks how many men will be needed and when Jordan seeks a place to hide explosives.

Jordan considers it a bad sign that he has forgotten Anselmo's name. It might mean simply that he's upset with himself for forgetting a significant piece of information. But it could also mean that he's uneasy about an invisible force at work in the situation. As you read, look for other references to fate and signs.

While Jordan waits, Anselmo goes to inform "the others" of Jordan's arrival. Hemingway describes Jordan here as a man who "did not give any importance to what happened to himself." This may mean that he sees himself merely as a cog in the great wheel of some cause or idea.

The importance of the individual is a major theme in *For Whom the Bell Tolls*. Here you see Robert Jordan's original position in relation to this idea. Watch for signs of change.

As he waits for Anselmo, Jordan's reflections explain why he's here. He is to blow up a bridge in these mountains. He received the mission from General Golz, whom he addresses, communist style, in a flashback as "Comrade General." Jordan is capable of doing the job; his experience at demolition is considerable. But it's absolutely crucial that the bridge be blown up at the precise moment the general attack that Golz is commanding has begun. Jordan will know from an aerial bombardment that the attack has started.

Two things are now clear: Jordan is a *partizan*, a

non-Spanish volunteer doing guerrilla work behind enemy lines. Golz (a pseudonym) is a Soviet career officer.

NOTE: Foreign Involvement in the Spanish Civil War   The Spanish Civil War was far from an exclusively Spanish affair. The Republican cause attracted volunteers from some 50 nations, with the largest number coming from France and Germany. Most of these volunteers were recruited and organized into the International Brigades by European Communist parties. More than 80 percent of the volunteers were (unlike Robert Jordan) working class people. A major recruiting office was in Paris where one of the staff members was Josip Broz—who after World War II became President Tito of Yugoslavia. About one third of the volunteers lost their lives in Spain.

Listening to Golz's comments, you may wonder why he's here in Spain at all. If you've ever tried to help an individual or a group, and your efforts were actually frustrated by the very people you were trying to aid, you have an idea of how Golz seems to feel. "You know how those people are," he complains to Jordan.

This won't be the first time you'll see uncomplimentary references to "those people," the very ones Golz and Jordan have come to help. It raises the question, Why do these two foreigners stay? Look for clues that answer this question and show you how Jordan and Golz really feel about the Spanish people.

NOTE: Many of Hemingway's friends (and one notable enemy, André Marty) appear in *For Whom the Bell Tolls*. Some bear their real names, such as the Loyalist commander Gustavo Duran and Petra, a chambermaid at the Hotel Florida where Hemingway stayed in Madrid. Others formed the basis for characters with fictional names. General Golz is closely based on the Polish general Karol Swierczewski. Karkov is the fictional name of the Soviet journalist and correspondent for the Soviet government newspaper *Izvestia*, Mikhail Koltsov. Hemingway often talked with Koltsov while in Spain during the civil war.

Pablo, the leader of the guerrilla band, joins the two men. Jordan's introduction to Pablo does not go pleasantly. Rather than welcoming Jordan, Pablo treats him rudely and with suspicion. "Here no one commands but me," he states sullenly.

So it's shocking when the 68-year-old Anselmo gives him a stiff tongue-lashing full of earthy insults. Your first clue that Pablo is not fully in charge has come early.

Pablo's objection to the bridge operation is that it will draw attention to the presence of his people's camp, and they'll no longer enjoy their relatively safe hideout. But Pablo finally gives in, and the guerrillas agree to carry the dynamite. Jordan has passed the first hurdle. Note that the hurdle was someone on *his* side: one of the people he is in Spain to help.

Pablo is caught in an inner conflict. He has become less interested in the cause the guerrillas are fighting for than in the preservation of the horses he recently acquired. Now that he owns property for the first time, Pablo is afraid that the mission to blow up the bridge will endanger his possessions. For some people, Hemingway seems to be saying, the desire to fight for a principle lessens if the fight affects the person on a material level. Perhaps you've been in a position similar to Pablo's. It's easy to voice concern over an issue, less easy to sacrifice something you love for it.

To Jordan, Pablo's sadness indicates that he is "going bad"; that is, showing signs of being a traitor. At this point, the reason is not completely clear, but we sense Pablo can't be trusted. Jordan also reminds himself to be cautious if Pablo suddenly becomes friendly. That will mean he has made a decision. About what? Hemingway leaves you in suspense here.

CHAPTER 2

The three men arrive at the hideout. Rafael, a gypsy member of the guerrilla band, is even less respectful of Pablo than is Anselmo. But with Jordan, Rafael is friendly and good-natured, and Jordan enlists his loyalty.

Jordan is the replacement for a previous demolition expert named Kashkin, who died in a manner that Jordan knows but won't reveal. Kashkin had been getting nervous about his work and speaking in a way that was bad for morale. It makes you wonder if the tension-filled job will eventually get to Jordan as well.

There are seven men and two women in the band Jordan will be working with to blow up the bridge.

One of the women is an attractive girl named Maria, whom he meets as she serves the evening meal. Throughout the meal, the girl and he stare at each other. Previously, Jordan had told Golz that there was no time for girls when one was working for the Republican cause. It looks as though Maria could change his mind.

Is this section realistic? You could see it as evidence of how firmly Jordan's relationship with Maria takes hold right from the start. But some readers feel that Hemingway has painted Jordan too much like a young man easily infatuated by a beautiful face and body.

Anselmo and Rafael prepare Jordan to meet the second woman in the band, Pablo's mistress, Pilar. You learn from Anselmo and Rafael that she is part gypsy, reads palms, has a vicious tongue, and is generally crude—and also very protective of Maria. It was Pilar's idea to take Maria with them when they left the scene of a Nationalist train they had just dynamited. Maria had been a prisoner on the train.

Pilar lives up to her billing. In her first speech she uses some salty language and gives the unmistakable impression of being in charge. She hurls insults at both Rafael and Pablo.

She is neither pretty nor feminine, but, to Robert Jordan, she *is* likable. Pilar exhibits qualities most people find admirable: she is strong, honest, unpretentious. It is easy to know where she stands.

Pilar is anxious for Maria to be removed from the situation. Pablo, she says, is beginning to desire the girl. But Jordan's attraction to Maria, which Pilar has noticed, doesn't seem to stir any resentment or misgivings in Pilar.

Pilar is definitely in charge of the guerrillas, in fact if not in name. She and Jordan discuss the bridge operation. Although they're counting on the assistance of El Sordo, a neighboring guerrilla leader, additional good help may be hard to get. There will be no money or loot from the bridge, as there was from the train they had blown up. Instead, the operation will be dangerous and will make it necessary to move from the mountain hideouts.

Pilar asks to look at Jordan's hand. Remember she is a gypsy; and remember he has said he doesn't believe in the occult. Pilar sees something in Jordan's hand that she obviously doesn't like. But she won't tell what it is. And Jordan, the unbeliever who is "only curious," is frustrated at not knowing.

Notice the foreshadowing of doom that Hemingway suggests for Robert Jordan: Pilar's reluctance to tell him what his palm has told her and the revelation that Kashkin, Jordan's predecessor, is dead. Jordan refuses to pay attention to these signs, but you can look at them as Hemingway's hints that all will not go well for Jordan.

CHAPTER 3

Jordan and Anselmo go to inspect the bridge. But the details of the bridge are not Hemingway's real concern in this chapter. Through Jordan and Anselmo, the chapter offers a philosophical consideration of the necessity and the morality of killing.

The conversation between Robert Jordan and Anselmo gives you a good basis on which to develop your thoughts about the taking of someone's life. Although the two men are on the same side politically, their consciences are not the same. Jordan confesses a repugnance for killing animals, yet claims he feels nothing when it is necessary to kill a human being "for the cause." Anselmo has no problem with hunting and killing animals, but to him it's a sin to kill a man—"even Fascists whom we must kill."

Hemingway presents you with profound issues here early in the story. If something is *necessary*, can it be *sinful*—in other words, truly wrong and therefore blameworthy? Or do you proceed from the other end first: if something is truly sinful, can it possibly be truly necessary? Your own religious background and ideas of morality will certainly affect your analysis and opinion of this interchange between Jordan and Anselmo.

Jordan's original position on the importance of the individual compared to the cause is reinforced again. "You are instruments to do your duty," he reflects, speaking of himself and others like him.

Certainly you can think of situations where individuals are part of a team effort and times when doing one's duty is necessary to the group's success and is a praiseworthy, honorable thing to do. Team sports are an obvious example.

But how far does this value of "duty" extend? How much sacrifice of self is ever necessary? *For Whom the Bell Tolls* raises these questions eloquently.

NOTE: Religion and the Spanish Civil War The historical relationship between the Roman Catholic Church and the government of Spain has been complex and stormy. Because a vast majority of the Spanish people has long been Catholic, the Church has had great power in the country. In the 1930s, as Spaniards began to divide into various political groups that leaned to the right or to the left, the Church aligned itself with the right. In the election of 1936 the left offered political amnesty to many anarchists and other political prisoners known to be anti-Church. This, plus the strong support of religious values by the right, prompted the Church to favor the Nationalist cause. As a result, many churches were burned and many clerics murdered by leftist fringe groups, and the Republican government did little to stop them, an attitude that further widened the gap between the Church and the left.

The victims of this schism mainly were the Spanish peasants. Marxist theories that urged them to forget God and espouse atheism were accepted by some, but many could not expel their religious beliefs so easily. The concept of sin and a life hereafter as a reward for a good life could not be ignored. Anselmo poignantly represents this conflict.

As they approach the camp, Jordan and Anselmo meet Agustín, one of the guerrilla band. Agustín is guarding the entrance to the camp, but he has forgotten the password— a clear indication that this is not the best prepared of rebel groups. Watch for Agustín to be one of the fiercest anti-Monarchist rebels, a man with little trust for any-

one. Here he warns Jordan to guard the dynamite—from Pablo.

CHAPTER 4

In some ways, Chapter 4 is like the classic scene
from a Western movie where two men confront
each other in a war of nerves that may soon turn
into a war of bullets.

The showdown between Pablo and Robert Jordan begins. It soon becomes a matter of Pablo ver-
sus everyone else. At stake are two things: demolition of the bridge and official leadership of the
guerrilla band. Hemingway builds the tension with
mastery. Death for one of the men looms as a real
possibility.

In the end, Pablo loses on both accounts. After
a moment so tense that Jordan's hand is resting
on his pistol, Pablo officially backs down and re-
linquishes command to Pilar. The remaining guerrillas endorse the demolition of the bridge, but only
after Pilar approves of it.

Notice that there is less than unanimous commitment among the gypsies to the mission of de-
stroying the bridge. Most would rather blow up a
train, which at least would result in material to
loot. One of them says that the bridge means nothing, that he is "for the *mujer* of Pablo," and others
agree. The somewhat indifferent attitudes of these
men emphasize one of Hemingway's themes: that
the Spanish Civil War was fought in large part for
the leaders of Spain and of foreign countries, not
for the people of Spain, who had the most to lose.
Here, Hemingway shows you a band of rebels doing

their best to get along, although not sure why they're fighting.

Hemingway also dwells on the relationship of the individual to mankind and mysticism, both through Pilar. Pilar shows a devotion to the cause similar to Jordan's with her statement, "I am for the Republic, and the Republic is the bridge." The personal consequences of the demolition of the bridge, she claims, mean nothing to her.

Secondly she states, "That which must pass, will pass." And upon remembering what she saw when she read Jordan's hand, she becomes at first momentarily enraged—and then extremely sad. The chapter leaves us wondering what Pilar knows that we don't.

CHAPTER 5

At the opening of this chapter, in the sentence beginning, "There was no wind . . . ," Hemingway gives us still another typical Hemingway description: a single sentence almost 180 words long, detailing the sights and smells of the cave and contrasting them with the sights and smells of the night outside the cave. Notice again the preponderance of nouns.

Jordan finds from Rafael that in the preceding tense scene the band had both expected *and wanted* him to kill Pablo.

And then Pablo returns—full of friendliness and welcome! You may remember that Jordan had warned himself at the end of Chapter 1 to be wary if Pablo ever became friendly.

The chapter concludes with Pablo delivering a maudlin, drunken soliloquy to one of the horses.

This is a good opportunity for you to examine your opinion of Pablo. Is he more to be despised or to be pitied? Why?

CHAPTER 6

Pilar and Robert Jordan develop instant rapport. She openly encourages his appreciation of Maria's charm. Pilar quickly sees that Jordan may be what Maria needs to heal the wounds left by her captors.

Two more things emerge from this short chapter. Pilar does not see danger in Pablo's weakness, as Jordan does. And Maria needs a man. She cultivates Jordan's attention; in a low-keyed manner, she practically flirts with him.

Jordan is upset when Pilar jokingly addresses him by the aristocratic title "Don." It seems to offend his democratic sensibilities. In the course of their conversation, Jordan asserts that he is not a communist; he is simply an antifascist. In this statement, Jordan may be reflecting Hemingway's own beliefs.

CHAPTER 7

Chapter 7 marks the beginning of Jordan and Maria's love relationship. Since this relationship will be one of the main strands of the story, the chapter is particularly significant.

Robert Jordan is asleep in his robe beyond the mouth of the cave. He is awakened by Maria. She protests a bit about getting into the robe with him, but not much. After all, she came there of her own volition.

This is the first but not the last such episode of lovemaking for these two. Maria reveals that she has been sexually used before—"things were done to me"—by her Nationalist captors, but that was not lovemaking. And she is not "sick" (from a sexually transmitted disease).

Today's novels are filled with graphic descriptions of sexual encounters. Hemingway couldn't go that far in 1940. Whether he would have, if it had been possible, is an unanswerable question. Most readers feel that his version is poetic and tasteful. It focuses more on the lovers' dialogue and feelings than on a clinical description of lovemaking.

NOTE: Some readers have pointed to this scene as wildly unrealistic. Given the morals of the day and of the country, no single woman would be so brazen as to give herself so openly to a relative stranger. Others defend Hemingway's choice, saying that Maria's behavior is necessary in order to accelerate the love affair between them. Within the space of less than three days she must offer him a love relationship that will help bring about a change in the way he perceives the war and his role in it.

CHAPTER 8

This chapter contrasts sharply with Chapter 7. It's concerned completely with the war and Jordan's assignment to demolish the bridge.

As Jordan's second day begins, a huge number of enemy planes are roaring overhead. He listens for the sound of bombs. By noting the lapse of time between the planes flying overhead and the sound of the bombs, he could then calculate where the lethal missiles were being dropped.

But no bombs are dropped. The planes are not attacking. A terrible possibility strikes him: a large force of planes are being assembled because the Nationalists *expect* a Loyalist attack!

His premonition becomes more likely. Fernando, who was in La Granja the previous night, reports rumors of a Loyalist attack . . . including the demolition of a bridge! La Granja is a Nationalist town—how could there be such a drastic leak in security?

CHAPTER 9

This is an important chapter that offers, principally through dialogue, insights into Pilar, Pablo, and Jordan.

Pilar confesses a "sadness" to Jordan. It's actually a despair she feels: death is on the way for many. In previous times, she would have shared this feeling with God. Now, as a communist, she cannot. Yet she confesses that God probably still exists, "although we have abolished Him."

Her conversation also reveals how much Pablo is hurting. He is deeply wounded that the group sided against him. And he's afraid to die. He clings to his one great moment of glory, the assault on the train. You may find this revelation little more than the tearful carrying-on of a man who has lost his courage. Or you may see it as a pitiful cry for help from a man broken by inner torment and the demands of war.

Agustín, one of Pablo's band, doesn't see Pablo as completely broken, though. He's convinced they'll need Pablo's skills when they retreat after the bridge is blown. Pablo may currently be a coward, but he is nonetheless "smart," according to Agustín. Pilar—for all her bravery, loyalty, decisiveness, intuition, and heart—is not "smart."

Exactly what he means by "smart" is something of a mystery at this point. Is he referring to Pablo's skills in conducting guerrilla maneuvers, and, if so, will those skills really be needed later on?

This chapter contains brief references to the themes of hypocrisy and mysticism. When Pilar asks Jordan if he has faith in the Republic, he answers yes—and *hopes* his answer is true. Is his devotion to the cause weakening? In that case, is he a hypocrite for answering yes?

And Jordan, the practical demolition expert, is still worried about what Pilar saw in his hand. Pilar calls the palmreading "nonsense." But she doesn't really mean that. She says it because telling what she saw might harm the Republic. Is she being a hypocrite too, lying and denying reality (as she saw it) for the sake of this supposedly glorious cause?

CHAPTER 10

This chapter is notable for its gruesomely graphic account of a Loyalist takeover of a Nationalist town, complete with barbaric ritual executions. Pilar relates the incidents to Jordan and Maria as the three of them make their way to El Sordo.

But Hemingway accomplishes two other purposes earlier in the chapter, before Pilar's gory account begins.

With one exception (relaying her "sadness" to Jordan) we've seen Pilar only as a strong, practical leader who wants to get the business of war done. But on the way to El Sordo, it's Pilar who wants to stop and rest, take in the beauty of the surroundings, and bathe her feet in a stream. So even Pilar, the strong, rough-hewn woman soldier, has a side that wants to be an ordinary person, enjoying simple things like the rush of cold water across bare feet.

Pilar is ugly—so much so that she cannot risk going to a Fascist city. She's known to be a Loyalist, and her exceptional ugliness makes her instantly noticeable. Her reflections of what it's like to be ugly on the outside but to feel beautiful on the inside make a poignant scene. In spite of her ugliness, Pilar has not lacked for lovers. She recites the cycle of each relationship. At first, love blinds both the man and herself to her unattractiveness. Then, "for no reason," the man notices the ugliness. He leaves, no longer blind. And neither, anymore, is the woman. She realizes all over again that she is ugly.

In Pilar's story of the Loyalist assault on a Nationalist town, we see a completely different Pablo. He is energetic, decisive, aggressive—and almost unbelievably cruel. Can you imagine these qualities in the Pablo you've seen so far? If so, what is it that you've noticed in the usually drunk and "cowardly" Pablo that makes it easy to believe he could have been aggressive and cruel?

With Pablo in charge, the Loyalists took over the Nationalist barracks. The wounded were killed outright. Four soldiers remained. In a stroke of irony, Pablo got instructions from one of them on how to use the Mauser pistol he had taken from a dead officer. Then he made them kneel and calmly killed each of them with it.

But Pablo wanted more than the slaughter in the barracks. He wanted to taste revenge and blood, and to hear the screaming of the town's Fascist sympathizers as they were savagely beaten before dying. These prominent men of the town had been seized in their homes at the same time the assault on the barracks had begun. Then they were taken to the town hall and kept there.

Pablo organized the town square as if for a celebration. Citizens were arranged in two lines leading from the door of the town hall to the edge of a cliff. Each was given a flail.

NOTE: A flail is an old-fashioned tool for hand-threshing grain. It consists of a long staff with another shorter and thicker pole attached at the end of the staff by a hinge or a heavy cord so that it can swing freely. The damage to a human body from a strongly wielded flail would be considerable.

One by one, the fascists were taken from the town hall and made to run the gauntlet of the flailing lines. The citizens who had instruments even more torturous and lethal than flails (such as sickles and pitchforks) were put at the end of the gauntlet, by the cliff. This was to prevent any of the fascists from being killed too soon—before they made it through the entire line.

At first the peasants were uncertain; this was not their idea. But as one man after another came from the town hall and went staggering to his death, they became cruel. They began to enjoy it.

They were drinking, of course, but Pilar says they were overcome by a drunkenness caused by something other than wine, a "drunkenness" that comes from great ugliness.

Perhaps the ultimate in ugliness came with the execution of Don Guillermo, a fascist storeowner. Pilar points out that he at least should have been executed quickly and with dignity. He was a fascist in name only, and his wife had remained a Catholic. Ironically, the flails and other tools that the peasants were using came from his store.

Yet, with his wife watching and screaming, Don Guillermo was brutally killed before he even got to the edge of the lines and the cliff.

And then the situation became even uglier. Impatient with waiting for the men to be released one by one from the town hall, the mob stormed the building and attacked the remaining fascist prisoners in a slashing frenzy of sickles and pitchforks and reaping hooks.

Pablo sat calmly watching.

They had taken the town. But Pilar was disgusted with the brutality. As for Pablo, he "liked it . . . all of it."

This chapter has been described as assaulting the reader with its explicit ugliness. Beyond question it's powerful. But it's also a puzzle. The Spanish Civil War was filled with atrocities committed by both sides. Yet in the one chapter that describes

such a scene, Hemingway chose to feature sense-
less, inhumane brutality committed by the side he
himself favored: the Republic.

He even crowns it with a pathetic yet ludicrous
scene. A drunken Loyalist pours wine over a dead
body and tries to set it afire. Failing, he finally
gives up the attempt, drinks the remaining wine
instead, and sits in a stupor patting the dead body.

Why put your own side in such a bad light?
Obviously, it shows us a very different Pablo. Per-
haps Hemingway wanted to show that his book
was objective despite his close ties to the Loyalists.
Both sides are capable of atrocities, not just the
Nationalists.

NOTE: Terrorism and atrocities occur in almost
any war. There were many during the Spanish Civil
War, although reports were sometimes sensation-
alized and exaggerated in the press. Republicans
and Nationalists were equally guilty, but each side
tended to excuse its behavior on grounds that
atrocities committed by the other side were worse.
The incident recounted by Pilar in Chapter 10 is
based on actual events in the city of Ronda (near
Málaga), where victims were thrown over cliffs.

CHAPTER 11

This chapter is linked closely to Chapter 10 in
questioning the merits of war. The repulsively brutal picture presented in Chapter 10 is now followed
by more intellectual considerations. Chapter 11 is
significant because it begins another central strand

in the story: the change in Robert Jordan's attitude toward what he is doing here in Spain.

At El Sordo's camp, Jordan, Pilar, and Maria are met by young Joaquín, who was part of the train operation. Joaquín was also there—crying and unwilling—when Pablo took over the town and engineered the brutal executions. Joaquín's family themselves had been executed by the fascists.

This knowledge and the effect of listening to Pilar's story bring some reflections that you may find startling to be coming from Robert Jordan:

The war isn't helping these people. *Partizans* such as himself come into an area, perform their missions, and leave; then the people of the area suffer reprisals—often death—as a result.

Although Jordan automatically speaks of the fascists and Nationalists as "barbarians," his side commits atrocities too. He has always recognized that fact in an intellectual way. Now, Pilar has made him see it, feel it.

In spite of these realizations, Jordan postpones reconsidering his judgments about the value of the war. He returns to his belief that the war is all-important and reaffirms loyalty to his war-making duties. Later, he tells himself, *after* the war is won, he'll sort it out and make judgments based on his experience. But he's beginning to wish there wasn't quite so much experience.

Stop for a moment here and reevaluate your picture of Robert Jordan. Certainly he's not a fool. And certainly he has seen evidence that this war is not helping anyone and is not likely to. But as soon as these reflections begin to bother him, he returns to his position: we *must* win this war or all is lost. In contrast with his reflections, does the position seem simplistic? Is he backing away from the truth, unable to face it? Is his "Act now, think later" attitude an example of intellectual cowardice?

That's a possible explanation. But if so, Jordan is doing something we've all done at some time. Can you recall an occasion when you doggedly clung to a position in spite of mounting evidence that it was wrong or at least needed reevaluation?

Jordan's self-doubts are just the first of many he will have. Here he is made uncomfortable by his feelings and therefore turns to a more pleasant subject—Maria.

Was last night true or just a dream? Was it like the imaginary lovemaking he had engaged in with Greta Garbo and Jean Harlow, the sex goddesses of the movie world at that time?

This passage prompts various reactions. Some readers feel that it's realistic and we're getting an authentic look into the complex psyche of Robert Jordan. Others see the passage as juvenile and almost embarrassing, coming in the midst of a serious novel. What is your reaction as you read it?

Jordan finally gets to meet the partially deaf guerrilla leader that he'll be relying on to help blow the bridge. El Sordo is strange but hospitable. (His nickname means "The Deaf One;" his real name is Santiago.)

With offhand remarks, both El Sordo and Pilar add to the sense of futility and approaching doom. El Sordo says that there are many people in the hills now, but fewer and fewer who are reliable. When Jordan suggests where Pilar and the guerrillas should go after the operation, Pilar becomes furious and tells him to let *them* decide what part

of the hills to die in. Again you see Jordan's uneasy
position as a foreigner come to Spain to help the
Republicans in the war. On some matters the
Spanish just don't want outside assistance or advice.

CHAPTER 12

This chapter sets the stage for the exceptionally
significant content of Chapter 13.

Jordan, Maria, and Pilar have secured the aid of
El Sordo, although he doesn't seem overly enthusiastic about giving it. On their way back, Pilar
stops to rest and reveals her affection for Maria,
even to the point of admitting that she herself is
somewhat jealous of Jordan.

But then she deliberately separates herself from
the pair and heads back to camp so that Jordan
and Maria can be alone. Maria seems extremely
anxious for this moment.

CHAPTER 13

You'll find a great deal to think about in Chapter
13. The relationship of Jordan and Maria is inten-
sified. Jordan entertains even more serious doubts
and recriminations about his activities in Spain and
begins to change his opinion of what is most important to him. You also learn a good bit more
about his background, which has been presented
sketchily so far.

Jordan and Maria's lovemaking was an intense
experience—both say they felt the earth move. Maria
confesses that she "died." Robert Jordan says he
almost did.

Jordan now realizes how special Maria is to him. He admits that he has made love before, but the earth did not move. There is magic in her body, he says.

Shortly afterwards, as they're walking back to meet Pilar, he begins planning the bridge operation. And suddenly he suffers from another wave of guilt and uncertainty about what he's going to do. These periods are coming more frequently now.

Jordan reflects ironically that he is about to do the kind of thing he is supposed to be fighting against, trying to prevent: he is about to use and at the same time destroy people. Why? He has to do this to help his side win the war. And why does he want his side to win? So that people don't get used and destroyed!

Yet, blowing up the bridge will not guarantee a successful end to the war, and it will certainly not help the people. So "should a man carry out impossible orders knowing what they lead to"?

Jordan's answer is yes. Yes, you must, because you won't know whether the orders are impossible (or harmful) until after you've executed the mission. Is Robert Jordan indulging in another instance of "Act now, think later"?

NOTE: Personal integrity vs. following orders
Although Jordan's orders come from General Golz, he wouldn't be court-martialed and ruined if he didn't carry them out; he's a skilled foreign volunteer, not a drafted recruit. But what do you think that someone in military or government service should do who believes that the orders from above are not only futile but harmful—perhaps even monstrously inhumane?

Can a person escape moral responsibility simply by saying, "I was following orders"? Are the personal consequences of not following orders (loss of job, ruination of career, imprisonment, perhaps even death) a valid consideration? Many high-ranking Nazis used "following orders" as a defense of their personal involvement in horrendous crimes during World War II.

Thoughts involving several of the novel's themes occupy Robert Jordan's mind now. He reflects that his presence brings danger to the people of the region. They'll be hunted down because of him. But, he rationalizes, if he weren't there, they'd be hunted down for some other reason anyway. So the war is futile, but it's still necessary to fight on.

He admits to himself that he has no particular politics now. This is amazing. A short while ago, he was saying that if this war (for people's rights) were lost, everything would be lost.

What's made the difference? Have his political views simply vanished, leaving a complete void? Not quite. Maria has come to fill the void.

He wants to spend the rest of his life with her. Consequently, he's no longer quite so enthusiastic about dying a hero's death as did the Greeks at Thermopylae, or holding out, like Horatius or the Dutch boy of legend, against almost insurmountable odds. Instead, he dreams of life with Maria as his wife back in the United States.

NOTE: Thermopylae was the name of the narrow mountain pass where the Greeks under the Spartan king Leonidas made a stand in 480 B.C. against invading Persians.

Horatius was a legendary Roman hero celebrated for his defense of a bridge across the Tiber against the Etruscans.

"The Dutch boy" is the hero of the tale that pictures him undertaking a night-long ordeal of plugging a small hole in a dike with his finger to prevent the hole from enlarging and causing the eventual collapse of the dike.

This section finally gives us answers to a few questions you've probably had about the background of Robert Jordan. He's a professor of Spanish at the University of Montana and has taken a leave of absence in 1937. He had spent much time in Spain during previous summers, doing civil engineering work, in the course of which he learned the science of demolition.

Now Jordan's thoughts occur rapid-fire. He realizes that bringing Maria home to the United States as his wife is a highly unlikely eventuality. But what he does have is *now*.

Is he being cheated if all he has is now? He tries hard to convince himself that a short time packed full of intense experiences could be the equivalent of living out a long life. And then he says that all such thoughts are nonsense.

Hemingway presents quite a picture of Robert Jordan: as a college professor, as a trained guerrilla and demolition expert, as an avid lover . . . and as a man who is very confused about the meaning of everything.

NOTE: Many readers have criticized Robert Jordan for being muddleheaded about his politics, saying that he hasn't learned enough about the issues to warrant leaving his university life to join the guerrilla band. According to these readers, he also makes many contradictory statements concerning his political philosophy, at one point saying he is merely an antifascist, at another point claiming to have no politics. Some readers defend Jordan, however, indicating that he is typical of many who supported the Republicans. Such people displayed much courage but often did not have a clearheaded intellectual understanding of the issues. As you read *For Whom the Bell Tolls* you'll want to consider whether Jordan is a contradictory person or whether his political beliefs are less important to his makeup than his heartfelt zeal.

Jordan and Maria find Pilar feigning sleep when they come back. Pilar seems to find vicarious satisfaction in learning (through insistent questioning) that the lovemaking was quite an experience for both Jordan and Maria.

Looking at the sky, Pilar predicts snow, even though it's late May. A snowfall could be disastrous for the guerrillas. Making a safe retreat after blowing up the bridge would then probably be more difficult than the demolition itself. If the snow-covered ground betrays their retreating tracks . . .

CHAPTER 14

Chapter 14, though short, is important for plot development and character revelation. Plans for blowing up the bridge receive a setback, Pablo becomes more of a villain, Jordan does some more philosophizing, and we learn quite a bit about Pilar's background.

It is late on the second day when Jordan, Pilar, and Maria return to the hideout. And it's snowing.

Jordan is furious. The job is difficult enough without the extra burden of freakish weather. Pablo, on the other hand, is positively enjoying the snow, or at least giving that impression. Remember, he doesn't want the bridge blown up. It'll ruin his security here in these hills. We can't tell whether he's gleefully anticipating calling off the operation or just perversely enjoying the bad luck of the people who are engineering the mission.

After fuming at the snow, Jordan returns to the composure and philosophy expected of a Hemingway hero. What if there is snow? What if the task is a little difficult? Calm down, stop complaining, and get the job done.

A great deal of the latter part of the chapter is devoted to Pilar's former lover, Finito. She reminisces about him, a relatively mediocre bullfighter who gathererd quite a following nonetheless by his brave manner in the ring.

NOTE: Bullfighting   To many people bullfighting is almost synonymous with Spanish culture. Beyond question, it is Spain's best-loved sport. Spectacle is perhaps a better word than sport, for in bullfighting, unlike conventional sports, there is little doubt of the outcome between the combatants, the matador and the toro. It is an elaborately staged drama comprising three acts, and the script calls for the bull to die. Bullfighting has been compared to ballet, for the bullfighter executes definite, stylized movements. An essential attraction of the spectacle is the courage of the matador, who places himself in a dangerous position from which he can emerge only with much skill.

Why is all this time spent on Finito, a character who is long dead when the story opens and who does not affect the plot in even a minor way? Pilar tells us that Finito was always fearful before a bullfight. Yet during the fight he did what he had to do and even distinguished himself. What he got for all this was the respect of a few people, a severely broken body, and a partly broken spirit.

He gave bullfighting his best effort . . . and ended by publicly coughing up blood as he stared in terror at the head of a bull.

What is Hemingway trying to tell us? Perhaps that even if defeat is inevitable, a person should behave honorably. Keep Finito's story in mind as Robert Jordan's story continues to unfold.

CHAPTER 15

It's now the second night after Robert Jordan's arrival. Most of this chapter features Anselmo at his post, noting the traffic on the road as Jordan has instructed him. He does a good job of keeping tabs on the number of vehicles, but doesn't distinguish the types of cars, as Jordan would have. There are many luxury vehicles, indicating a high concentration of top-level staff. You know from this fact that something is brewing. But Anselmo doesn't realize it and neither does Jordan.

Hemingway offers the reader this insight by a combination of omniscient point of view and direct statement. He relates a fact and then bluntly says, "But Anselmo did not know this" and "Robert Jordan would have . . ."

The main function of this chapter, however, is to collect the strands of several themes. Anselmo seems the perfect choice of a vehicle for the task. Throughout, Hemingway has emphasized Anselmo's straightforwardness and integrity.

Across the road is the sawmill. In it are enemy soldiers. *Evil* enemy soldiers? Not as Anselmo sees them. They are not even really fascists; they are simply men who have been forced to serve in the Nationalist army. Who are they then?

Individual men, just like himself: "It is only orders that come between us." Anselmo's only grudge against them is that they are warm and he is not. He hopes he won't have to repeat the killing and the cruelty that he's been part of in the past (back in "the great days of Pablo"). And he sums it up simply and poignantly: "I wish I were in my own house again and that this war were over."

Now Hemingway takes you into the sawmill itself, and we see the men just as Anselmo had pictured them. They're ordinary people with ordinary concerns, not monsters—although the war will no doubt make them capable of such a transformation.

It's an amiable scene. The soldiers realize they have an easy detail and wonder how long it will last. They're confident of the power of the Nationalist air force.

NOTE: Anselmo refers to the soldiers in the saw-mill as *Gallegos*, indicating that they are from Galicia, a region in the far northwest of Spain. The climate there is generally wet, but snow is rare. Anselmo wonders what they must think of snow—another facet of seeing them as ordinary human beings.

Galicians speak a distinctive dialect similar to Portuguese. From the men's speech, Anselmo could tell where they came from.

After letting us see the Galician Nationalists as simple human beings, Hemingway returns to An-selmo, who is doing still further soul-searching. More and more he regrets that any killing has to be done at all.

And here comes the moral paradox again: An-selmo says that the killing, even though necessary, is a great sin. (Can a genuine sin ever be neces-sary?) He decides there will be a need for penance after the war is over. God has been abolished by the Republicans, so a religious penance will be im-possible. Perhaps a civil penance of some sort will suffice. Even without God as a source and judge of morality, Anselmo feels the reality of evil and just as strongly feels the need to atone for it some-how.

NOTE: Atonement/Restitution   You might use this section to check your own feelings about atone-ment for wrongdoing. Do you think it's enough if a person has an honest change of heart and sin-cerely resolves not to repeat a wrong? Or must that be combined with additional action to make up for what was done?

Anselmo misses his prayers. He used to pray frequently but has not done so since the beginning of the movement. His reasons have nothing to do with a personal rejection of God. Ironically, they're rooted in Anselmo's own simple integrity: he figures that praying would be unfair and hypocritical. Under the Republic's official atheism, none of the others on his side are saying prayers . . . and he doesn't want special treatment anyway!

What a strange and tragic conflict stirs within Anselmo, a deeply religious man whose very integrity keeps him from practicing the religion he misses so much!

The pangs of guilt over the killing will not leave him. He's further tortured by the unresolvable dilemma of "necessary evil" and returns again to the concept of atoning for the sins of the war. He sees these sins as things that need to be removed from a man's soul.

Anselmo has been called the novel's "yardstick of humanity," suggesting that he is the ideal of moral stability by which the other characters should be measured. Anselmo is thoughtful, brave, loyal, and one of the few characters in the story concerned about the penance they will have to do for the killing and destruction of the war. As the eldest character, 68-year-old Anselmo may represent Hemingway's view that wisdom comes with age. In any case, he is one of the more admirable characters of *For Whom the Bell Tolls* and shows how much Spain lost when it wasted the resource of its people.

Robert Jordan arrives to bring Anselmo back from his observation post. Hemingway gives us a brief glimpse of the comradeship between them. Jordan knows that he can count on Anselmo. And perhaps on Fernando too. But that's not many, considering the task ahead.

CHAPTER 16

Back at the cave, Pablo is drunk, and Maria is waiting on Robert Jordan, trying to anticipate his every need.

El Sordo has come, leaving a bottle of whiskey as a present specifically for Jordan; then he's gone to look for the horses they'll need on the retreat after the bridge. The whiskey is a rare gift for the time and situation, and Jordan is grateful.

Now Pablo begins to suffer severe guilt pangs. He regrets the violence and killing he was responsible for when the movement began. He wishes he could restore his victims to life. It's highly uncertain, though, whether Pablo or Pablo's wine is delivering these repentant sentiments.

The others make conversation with Jordan, partly out of embarrassment for Pablo's drunkenness. They ask him questions about the United States and learn that he taught Spanish there. They are probably interested but also want to fill an embarrassing gap.

Pablo keeps entering the conversation. And he keeps insulting Jordan, particularly with immature insults about the latter's masculinity. Jordan begins to think that Pablo may not be as drunk as he appears—or wants to appear. It's a repeat of an earlier scene: an opportunity for Jordan to kill Pablo. Only now Jordan is more aware of the situation and has more incentive. He realizes more than before how dangerous Pablo could be to his operation.

And so he deliberately insults Pablo, hoping for some movement from the former leader that will justify a fatal retaliation of some sort, something that could be chalked up to self-defense. But Pablo senses a trap (which he's convinced Pilar has engineered) and will not walk into it.

Agustín takes the initiative with lurid insults and harsh slaps across Pablo's face. Still Pablo will not fight back. Moreover, he seems to know that he'll be needed during the retreat; he taunts Jordan with the prospect of having to lead the band to safety.

Pablo also makes a significant comment about the value of this ideological war and the merit of foreign involvement. He calls the band "a group of illusioned people" and refers to Jordan as "a foreigner who comes to destroy you."

Clearly, Pablo no longer feels allegiance to the Republic. In fact, such allegiance to the cause is precisely the illusion he's talking about. As for Jordan being a destroyer, that may be a little difficult to prove. He's about to destroy a bridge; we don't have any direct evidence that he has ever destroyed lives. On the other hand, it is difficult to see how he has saved or improved any lives.

Is Pablo right? Does this often drunken, superficially weak, less-than-admirable man have the best grasp on reality? As Pablo leaves to look after the horses, he needles Jordan again by pointing out that the snow is still falling.

CHAPTER 17

Prompted by Pilar, the guerrillas concur that Pablo is a danger and should be killed. Jordan agrees to shoot him. A tense scene ensues when Pablo suddenly reenters the cave. The planned assassination is about to take place when Jordan realizes that he can't shoot inside the cave—the dynamite is stored there.

But Pablo now shows a complete personality change. He maintains he's no longer drunk and says he wants to be involved in the demolition of the bridge. He even openly admits that he knows they have thought of killing him but stresses that only he can lead them to safety in the Gredos Range.

Pilar attributes the change in Pablo to his having overheard the plans to kill him.

Do you recall Jordan's suspicions about Pablo at the end of Chapter 1? Agustín's anger at the guerrillas for not killing Pablo suggests that Pablo may still be a threat to them.

CHAPTER 18

Most of this chapter contains Jordan's reflections about Gaylord's, a hotel in Madrid occupied by Soviet communists who had come to fight for the Republic. It's partly a story of the first stages in Robert Jordan's disillusionment. At Gaylord's "you learned how it was all really done instead of how it was supposed to be done."

At Gaylord's he had met the well-known "peasant leaders" of the Loyalist troops. Although they *were* originally simple peasants and workers, more recently they had spent time at the military academy in the Soviet Union and have Soviet interests at heart at least as much as Spanish interests. Jordan consoles himself that perhaps this manufactured peasant image isn't so bad because real peasant leaders, lacking the necessary military training, might very likely be more like Pablo.

NOTE: The three "peasant leaders" Jordan refers to in particular were Enrique Lister, a former stonemason; Juan Modesto, a former cabinetmaker; and Valentín Gonzalez, known as *El Campesino* ("The Peasant"). They were well trained, able military leaders.

The second of Jordan's disillusionments is with the luxuries that surrounded these communist leaders. (Communism was supposed to eliminate economic distinctions and privileges of class.) For a while, he had been able to accept this lifestyle on the part of his heroes (at least while they were at Gaylord's) and to give up the idea that champions of the common people should do without nice things. But the purity of revolutionary feeling dies fast, Jordan now reflects—for him within six months.

At Gaylord's, Jordan meets Karkov, a Soviet journalist who is more than just a reporter, and who serves somewhat as Jordan's tutor in the ways of this war.

Although Karkov is a minor character, he is compelling and interesting. Karkov is a realist. He holds no grand ideas about the qualities of the Loyalist forces. In a sense, he bares the reality of the Republican cause to Jordan.

Particularly significant is a comment Jordan makes to Karkov at one point: "My mind is in suspension until we win the war." You might see this as evidence that Jordan had adopted an "Act now, think later" stance long before taking the bridge assignment and meeting Maria.

NOTE: While covering the war in Spain, Hemingway stayed at the Hotel Florida when in Madrid. But he frequently called at Gaylord's, the Soviet center. He came and went freely there, although in many ways he disliked the place. Jordan's reactions to Gaylord's are basically Hemingway's: he felt it boasted too many luxuries, including gourmet food and drink, while the common people (on whose behalf they were supposed to be fighting) suffered. Nevertheless, he visited Gaylord's often in hope of gaining information about the war. There he frequently conversed with Mikhail Koltsov, a young Soviet journalist who appears in the book as Karkov.

CHAPTER 19

This is one of the few chapters that deals almost exclusively with only one theme. Here the theme is mysticism—knowledge gained by extraordinary, subjective means. It's been hinted at several times before, beginning with Pilar's reading of Jordan's palm.

The occasion of the theme is Kashkin, the demolition expert who preceded Jordan. Pilar claims she could foresee his impending doom. Jordan maintains that Kashkin simply lost his nerve and was afraid, and that it showed on his face.

Pilar then goes beyond appearances and says her gypsy nature could *smell* the death that was about to happen to Kashkin. Notice the components that Pilar says make up the smell of death. Her list is morbid and repugnant.

Jordan is distantly respectful of her lore. Comments from members of the band, however, suggest that this is a bit too much for them to accept, and Pilar seems to feel insulted.

There's nothing mystic about the danger to El Sordo, which Robert Jordan notes at the end of this chapter. The snow has stopped. But it's cold; the snow will stay on the ground. If El Sordo and his men have been out stealing horses for the retreat, they'll be easy to track down.

CHAPTER 20

But Robert Jordan and Maria aren't even *trying* to cover their traces on this second night since Jordan arrived at the scene of his assignment. Maria simply leaves the cave and goes outside to Jordan's robe-sleeping bag, even though the others are still awake.

Jordan has prepared a bed of pine boughs under the robe. Again they make love.

It's not the same as it was that afternoon—no earthquakes, no stirrings that shake the center of their beings. Yet Maria says she loved it more. "One does not need to die," she tells Jordan. He doesn't seem to have regrets either.

Is there something to learn here about the nature of human experience? Is it that we need only one intense experience to give meaning to all similar ones?

Jordan feels that Maria's body next to his is an alliance against death. What is the significance of this phrase? How can they together defeat death? Think in terms of the meaning, quality, and value of experience as Hemingway sees it, regardless of the calendar years (or even clock hours) a particular experience may comprise.

And yet, does this brave theory make Jordan any more willing to relinquish Maria, because they've shared an intense, "worth a lifetime" experience? He holds her "as though she were all of life and it was being taken from him." But he makes sure his pistol is handy.

CHAPTER 21

This extremely brief chapter abruptly jolts Robert Jordan from his lover/philosopher role and returns him to being a man of action.

His third day in the mountains begins early and dramatically. While still in the sleeping robe with Maria, he hears a horseman approaching. He waits. When the man comes into view, Jordan sees from his uniform that he's an enemy soldier and fires at him.

The slain cavalryman is probably part of a random patrol, but this means the enemy is in the area. Everyone is aroused instantly.

Now, perhaps predictably, the old Jordan takes over. Maria has "no place in his life now." He is once again the trained, efficient, deadly *partizan*, fighting for . . . what? This is a good place for you to attempt an answer. Answer first for yourself;

then answer as Jordan might have at this point in the story. But keep in mind that a few hours ago Maria was "all of life" to Robert Jordan, instead of having no place in it. Now when she wants to be with him, he orders her back. Robert Jordan is pure soldier at this point. He takes charge, orders the submachine gun to be set up on the hill, and gives instructions on its correct positioning and use. If the cavalryman is missed and if others follow his horse tracks (there's still enough snow on the ground), the guerrillas may have to make a stand. If this happens, it will likely ruin the bridge operation before it gets started. The enemy isn't supposed to know they're in the area until after the bridge has been destroyed.

CHAPTER 22

Chapter 22 resumes the action of the previous chapter without a moment's lapse or even a slight change of location. Jordan, Primitivo, and Agustín are installing the machine gun.

Into the midst of this situation comes a grinning Rafael, the gypsy, who has just killed two rabbits. He's proud of his accomplishment. That's not all bad: the band does need food, assuming they can escape from this situation. The upsetting part is that the enemy cavalryman came through the post Rafael was supposed to be watching. And the enemy might have heard the gypsy's gun shot.

The incident has symbolic significance. Before Rafael followed and killed them, the two rabbits were mating—"making love," if that term can be applied to rabbits. A few moments afterwards, they are dead. The foreshadowing is obvious if you remember that Jordan's nickname for Maria is "rab-bit."

Robert Jordan knows the pure mechanics of kill-ing and instructs his comrades. Shoot an officer first. Aim at the knees of a dismounted man if he is below you. Aim at the belly of a man if he is on a horse.

Primitivo is ready for some real action. He wants a massacre of the enemy. Jordan can't afford to condone Primitivo's bloodthirsty urges at this point, for fear of jeopardizing the bridge operation. So he appeases Primitivo with a simple message: Have patience . . . we'll have a massacre tomorrow at the sawmill and the roadmender's hut.

CHAPTER 23

Primitivo is above, at the lookout point; Agustín is by Jordan's side at the machine gun. Four enemy cavalrymen ride out of the timber, perfect targets. It's a rare chance to kill them with no chance of return fire—not from these four men anyway. Nevertheless, Jordan restrains himself: "But let it not happen."

Why not? Is it purely a judgment that gunfire would be foolhardy since others may be in the area? Or is his restraint mixed with some other motive?

Whatever the reason, it's a good professional move. Twenty more soldiers ride into and then out of view. If the first four had been killed, the twenty would have had to be dealt with.

A mild, comic-relief dialogue takes place be-tween Jordan and Anselmo about the placement of their official papers. It's necessary to carry of-ficial clearance papers for both sides when moving back and forth through the lines. In case of capture, the wrong ones must be swallowed.

To prevent a mixup, Jordan carries the Republican papers in his *left* breast pocket and the fascist papers in his *right* breast pocket.

Agustín, still a radical revolutionary (or still "illusioned," to use Pablo's viewpoint), complains that the Republic moves more to the "right" all the time. As evidence, he cites the fact that many Republicans are reinstating "Señor" and "Señora" to replace the equalizing term, "Comrade."

Agustín, Anselmo, and Robert Jordan present us with a variety of attitudes toward killing.

Agustín positively relishes the idea. He can't wait to get to it.

Anselmo, as we've seen, has killed because it was "necessary," but he regrets his actions. He openly opposes Agustín and maintains that *none* of the enemy should be shot. They should be reformed by work but not killed. He gives his position a philosophical backing: "Thus we will never have a Republic." By this expression, he seems to mean that killing simply for the satisfaction of wiping out the enemy will violate the very principles of individual human worth that the Republicans are supposed to stand for.

Jordan, by his own admission, is more like Agustín than Anselmo. He reflects, "We do it coldly but they do not," meaning that the *partizans* kill methodically, without emotion, but the Spanish have inherited their hot blood for killing. When they accepted Christianity, this urge was only suppressed, not wiped out. He even describes it as their "extra sacrament."

NOTE: In Roman Catholic theology, a sacrament is an action or event in which a believer encounters God. Baptism is the prime example. In this meeting, the believer's life is changed, enriched, made more meaningful. Hemingway's description of killing as "their extra sacrament" (the Catholic faith observes seven) is both eloquent and (to a Spanish Catholic) sacrilegious.

Then Jordan admits to himself that he *likes* to kill. Hemingway raises an important issue when he has Jordan say ". . . admit that you have liked to kill as all who are soldiers by choice have enjoyed it at some time whether they lie about it or not." Many readers point to such statements as proof that Hemingway endorsed warfare by talking of the "enjoyment" of it. Others contend that he is simply being frank about a reaction to war that has been well documented. How do you feel about Jordan's thoughts? Does Hemingway make war attractive in any way in *For Whom the Bell Tolls*? Or is it a frightening picture, made all the more terrible by the leading character admitting that there is pleasure to be had in taking the life of another?

Jordan cautions himself not to think of Anselmo as a typical Spaniard because Anselmo is a Christian, "something very rare in Catholic countries." This is a slight and/or sly jab at religion and particularly at Catholicism in Spain.

Again Hemingway is criticizing something he himself belonged to or supported. Previously, you've seen him present the Republic unfavorably in several instances. Now he does the same with the Catholic faith of which he was at least technically a member. (Hemingway was baptized a Catholic in Italy after sustaining such severe wounds in World War I that it seemed he might not survive. He remained nominally Catholic throughout his life and was buried in a Catholic ceremony at Ketchum, Idaho.)

CHAPTER 24

The enemy soldiers have gone; they didn't even know they were being watched. Now the band is having breakfast. There's a cheerful, lighthearted atmosphere, and the meal features such unlikely breakfast foods as wine and onions.

The breakfast scene at the guerrilla hideout seems like the scene at the campaign headquarters of a candidate who knows he or she is likely to lose. The defeat hasn't officially occurred yet, so the participants decide to make the best of their situation.

Then from a distance comes the sound of automatic rifle fire. They all realize what this means. El Sordo and his men have been detected and are defending themselves. Agustín wants to go to their aid immediately. Jordan says no: "We stay here."

CHAPTER 25

In Chapter 25, Hemingway hints even more strongly—through the characters themselves—at the probability of death for the band.

Primitivo can curse. That's nothing new to you by now. Most of the characters in this novel are blessed with very earthy, colorful tongues. But Primitivo's present cursing is not the nonchalant foul mouth of a man who disagrees with somebody.

His cursing is deliberate, serious, directed at the enemy. The group can hear the battle sounds of El Sordo's band being massacred. And so Primitivo curses and cries. Pilar is more hardened. She talks to Primitivo with contempt for such feelings and for wanting to go to El Sordo's aid. And then she says that Primitivo will die soon enough here with his own band—why make an unnecessary trip to die with others?

But Pilar comes down from her pedestal when an enemy plane roars overhead. Fearfully, she refers to it as the "bad luck bird." "For each one there is something," she says. "For me it is those." Do you also have a weak spot—a sight or a sound that automatically brings a pang of fear or at least uneasiness?

It's time to prepare the noon meal. The hares would taste better if they were cooked tomorrow or the next day, but Pilar says they might as well eat them today. And Jordan agrees. It's clear that they are aware of the possibility that none of them will still be around tomorrow.

CHAPTER 26

This chapter opens with a powerful consideration of the theme of killing and in so doing illustrates Robert Jordan's change in attitude.

That morning, Jordan had killed a young Nationalist cavalryman, an insignificant incident in military terms, and to Jordan, involving simply another one of the enemy.

But now Jordan is looking through the young man's papers. There's a letter from his sister, with news of his parents and his village. A second letter is from the soldier's fiancé, frantic with worry about his safety.

Suddenly Robert Jordan doesn't want to read any more of the man's letters. They're painful proof that this was not just another one of the faceless "them." This was a man—with a mother, a father, a sister, and a girl he loved.

Jordan reflects, in a line characteristic of Hemingway's irony, that you never kill anyone you want to kill in a war.

The dead soldier's letters lead Jordan into a lengthy interior monologue. Does he have a right to kill? Of course not. But he "must"—"necessary evil" again.

He has killed more than twenty people so far. Only two of them were fascists, so far as he knows. Thus, he concludes, he has actually been killing the very people he likes and wants to help: ordinary Spanish citizens.

But they oppose the cause. The cause is right. So he must kill in order to prevent something worse from happening. That bit of theory doesn't relieve his mounting guilt either. He tells himself to stop this train of thought. It's going to keep him from being a coldly efficient soldier.

What *does* Robert Jordan believe in? Not all the things he claims to believe, so that he can justify being here in this war, killing people. He finally admits this to himself.

Is Robert Jordan, the idealistic liberal and highly

educated American *partizan*, really Robert Jordan, the hyprocrite? Not too long ago, he reflected that secretly he enjoyed killing.

Then he says that above all else, love is the most important thing to a human being, whether it lasts for a long life or for just a day. Does he really believe that—or is he trying to make himself feel better about the next twenty-four hours?

CHAPTER 27

Up to this point scenes in which Robert Jordan is present have dominated the novel. The few exceptions include the scene in which Pablo talks to his horses at the end of Chapter 5 and the chapter in which Anselmo reflects on the enemy soldiers in the mill followed by a brief look inside the mill itself to listen to them. But Chapter 27 belongs completely to El Sordo.

This other guerrilla leader, so unlike Pablo, went to steal horses for the retreat after the bridge is blown up. The snow enabled the Nationalists to follow the guerrillas, and now they've been forced to make a defense on a hill.

There are five men left on the hilltop. Four are wounded, including El Sordo himself. They're in pain, and El Sordo ironically refers to death as an aspirin. He has shot to death one of the wounded horses and used the body to plug the gap between two rocks so that he can fire over it at the enemy.

Joaquín, the youngest in the group and the only remaining idealist, parrots the Communist slogan: "Hold out and fortify and you will win." The slogan evokes an expletive from one of his less "illusioned" comrades.

Joaquín tries another, "It is better to die on your feet than to live on your knees," but gets the same response.

NOTE: La Pasionaria Joaquín is quoting Dolores Ibarruri, a Communist heroine known as La Pasionaria. Always dressed in black, she made passionate pro-Republic speeches in Madrid, urging the people to resist Nationalist attempts to capture the city. "It is better to die . . . " began one of her most famous exhortations. She was greatly admired by the Loyalists. Yet the theme of hypocrisy emerges here when one of the guerrillas maintains that her own son is safely away in the Soviet Union.

El Sordo's men have killed some of the Nationalists who foolishly tried to storm the hill, but the guerrillas are doomed and know it. They can hold out for a while; however, the enemy needs only to bring a trench mortar (a short cannon for firing shells at a high angle) or send planes, and the battle will be over quickly.

Hemingway gives us an earthy image of the hill on which El Sordo and his men have been forced to make a defense. To El Sordo it looks like a chancre (an ulcer caused by syphilis) with themselves as the pus.

Dying is easy to El Sordo. He does not fear it. He can accept it. But he hates it. He has no glorious sacrificial view of death. Perhaps such a view can come only from those engaged in the *theory* of revolution—not from those engaged in the devastating details of waging such a war.

El Sordo tricks the enemy into thinking the men on the hill have committed suicide. The Nationalist soldiers try to determine if this is the case by baiting them with increasingly gross insults. Their captain (Hemingway lets us know he is not quite rational) stands atop a boulder in the open and dares someone to kill him.

No response.

The captain then strides up the hill. El Sordo is sad that only one enemy soldier will be killed by his ploy, but at least it's a major officer. Referring to his enemy as Comrade Voyager (on the journey to death), El Sordo shoots him. The Nationalists resume firing on the hill. But now the planes come too, and El Sordo begins his last stand. Hemingway's description makes it one of the most powerful episodes in the novel. Along with the rest of this chapter, it overflows with the themes of *For Whom the Bell Tolls*.

The droning of the planes has weakened the young Joaquín's idealistic bravado, but he still recites the slogans of La Pasionaria—until the planes get close.

Then Joaquín, the officially atheistic Communist, switches to the Hail Mary! When the planes are actually overhead, he interrupts his Hail Mary and begins the Act of Contrition, a prayer expressing sorrow for sin.

But the machine gun is roaring over his head and the enemy planes are roaring over the hill and Joaquín cannot remember the Act of Contrition. All he can remember is the final phrase of the Hail Mary: ". . . and at the hour of our death." Many readers see Joaquín's plight as one of the most moving in the entire novel. He is a classic victim of the Spanish Civil War, loyal to the Republican cause but still tied to his Catholic roots.

The planes do their job well. Very quickly there is no one left alive on the hill except an unconscious Joaquín. With the captain dead, Lieutenant Berrendo is in charge of the Nationalist troops on the hill. Within a few paragraphs, Berrendo displays a conflicting spectrum of conduct ranging from decency to butchery.

Finding Joaquín still alive, Berrendo makes the sign of the cross and "gently" shoots him. This may be seen as a humane act by the Lieutenant. But then he orders his men to cut the heads from the dead bodies and put them in a poncho to bring back for purposes of "proof and identification."

He prays for the soul of one of his own soldiers before leaving the scene because he doesn't want to see the beheading he himself has ordered.

CHAPTER 28

This short chapter stands as an epilogue to the previous one. It's the aftermath of El Sordo's doomed stand. Hemingway gives you a chance to think about it.

The Nationalist cavalry pass in front of Robert Jordan's eyes again. Jordan sees a long poncho "bulging as a pod bulges with peas." We know what's in there although Jordan doesn't yet.

Hemingway gives us another insight into the complex character of Lieutenant Berrendo. He feels distaste for what's just happened, yet he basically enjoys military maneuvers. He says a prayer to the Virgin Mary for his dead friend Julian.

Anselmo, returning from his duty of tallying vehicle movement, passes the hill where El Sordo made his final stand and sees the headless bodies. And now Anselmo prays, for the first time since the start of the movement; it is the same prayer Lieutenant Berrendo just said!

CHAPTER 29

This chapter introduces one of the final strands in the latter part of the novel: the mission of Andrés to deliver Jordan's letter to Golz.

Jordan and Pablo are sitting across a table from each other. Jordan is making notes; Pablo is getting drunk. It looks like business as usual.

But these aren't ordinary notes. Jordan is writing to Golz to inform him that the fascists know of the upcoming offensive. He feels it will not succeed or will not be worth the price. But he doesn't want to lose face. Golz must know that Jordan's reservations about the attack do not come from cowardice or timidity. We realize again that Jordan himself doesn't know what the overall plan *is*—and that it's possible the plan isn't even meant to succeed.

Andrés is selected to carry Jordan's communication across enemy lines to the Republican headquarters.

NOTE: The Military Information Service, represented by the S.I.M. seal that Jordan puts on his letter, was not a particularly admirable arm of the Republic. Organized to investigate deserters and opponents of the Republic, it became controlled by communists. Its success relied greatly on secret prisons and torture chambers.

CHAPTER 30

The buildup to the final action is interrupted in Chapter 30, which is devoted primarily to Robert Jordan's personal history.

Andrés has been gone three hours. Now we learn why Jordan has sent the message to Golz: Anselmo had brought information about a massive buildup of enemy equipment that was not supposed to be in the area at all.

Jordan greatly admires his grandfather, an excellent soldier who had fought in the U.S. Civil War. In fact, the grandfather is his masculine "father image." His own father committed suicide with the officer's pistol that belonged to Jordan's grandfather. Thus the weapon went, in Jordan's opinion, from noble to cowardly use. Afterwards, Jordan dropped it in a deep lake.

Jordan sees his father as a coward, first for being henpecked by Jordan's mother, but primarily for having committed suicide. In his thoughts he refers to his father as "that one" and "that other one that misused the gun."

Remember that Hemingway's own father committed suicide with a firearm. His father was suffering from both physical and financial problems, and at the time Hemingway did not display any condemnation or disgust at his father's action (although later he spoke of his father's "cowardice" as "the worst luck any man could have").

In an earthy reflection that might have come from one of the Spanish peasants he's working with, Jordan speculates that "the good juice" came through to him only after passing through his father. Then he cautions himself to count on good juice only if he's proved it by the end of tomorrow.

Even Jordan can see some irony in his situation. He admires his grandfather, who was so conservative that he never associated with Democrats—yet Jordan himself has been offered a chance to study at the Lenin Institute in Moscow!

CHAPTER 31

On this third night, Maria is unable to make love. She feels pain, which she attributes to "the things [that] were done" by her Nationalist captors. Instead of making love, they make plans to go to Madrid. They spin elaborately whimsical dreams of how they'll spend a month in a hotel room.

Many people have done what Maria and Robert Jordan are doing: planning things that will never happen. Can you remember a time when you've done the same thing—talked with somebody about a future that was either impossible or very unlikely?

At first Jordan enjoys the fantasizing. Then he realizes he's simply lying. He continues for Maria's sake, but it's no longer enjoyable.

Pilar has been fantasizing too, whether for her own sake or Maria's, by preparing Maria for her marriage role when she and Jordan return to the United States to live.

NOTE: Male/female roles   Are men dominant in *For Whom the Bell Tolls*? Some readers argue that Pilar disproves this. Others feel that she is only a rare exception. She leads only because Pablo has relinquished his natural dominance by drunkenness and cowardice. Yet this same strong, unmistakably-in-charge Pilar instructs Maria in wifely duties that many readers find subservient.

Although Jordan generally does not act in an excessively male-dominant manner, at times he is certainly condescending and talks down to Maria as though she were a child.

How does Jordan's behavior strike you? If you're female, does such behavior by a man bother you or do you accept it as simply part of the culture and the times? If you're male, do you find yourself wishing that man-woman relationships were like Jordan and Maria's—with the man dominant—or is it better when both partners are more equal?

Maria's father had been a Republican and the mayor of their village. Maria describes the execution of her parents by the Nationalists and her subsequent capture and rape. The story angers Jordan, and he's glad they'll be killing tomorrow.

And then he indulges in strange reasoning: when the Nationalists, the "flowers of Spanish chivalry," raped Maria, they knew better but acted deliberately and on purpose. *His* side has done very bad things too . . . but out of ignorance (or so he claims).

Is this the thinking of a mature college professor or of a little child? ("*I* couldn't help it, but *he* did it on purpose!") Is Robert Jordan a mixture of both?

Then he decides that being killed tomorrow doesn't matter as long as the bridge gets blown properly. Maybe he has experienced all of his life in these last three days.

CHAPTER 32

For the second time, Hemingway presents a complete chapter without Robert Jordan. The scene is Gaylord's, the Madrid hotel occupied by communist *partizans* and people of similar beliefs. These are the people who preach a classless society with no special advantages to any privileged group. They've come to Spain to help bring power and complete equality to the common people. Do they look and act like austere, dedicated freedom fighters? Not exactly. They eat well, drink well, and do not lack for sexual diversion. Living in the midst of a besieged capital city, they're enjoying parties. The contrast with the situation of people like Jordan and Maria is striking.

News of their Loyalist offensive scheduled for the following morning has spread throughout the area. The reaction at Gaylord's to this inexcusable, potentially fatal leak in security is laughter!

Once again we have to wonder why Hemingway painted his own side so bleakly. Remember that he was writing after the war had been lost by the Republicans, whom he favored. Perhaps he wanted to show that a noble cause died at the hands of less-than-noble leaders. In any case, here he describes one of the Republican inner circles as a group of overstuffed, self-important oafs who throw parties in a time of peril and use unfounded rumors to buoy their confidence.

An exception is the Soviet journalist Karkov, who

may represent Hemingway's own feelings. After talking with a few people at this pre-attack celebration, he retires to his room at Gaylord's, disgusted.

CHAPTER 33

It's 2:00 A.M., the middle of Jordan's third night. Pilar wakes him with bad news. Pablo has gone, deserted. That in itself isn't so bad; maybe they'll be better off without him. But Pablo took the detonation devices that Jordan needs to blow up the bridge. That *is* disastrous. Pilar is apologetic and guilt-ridden. She feels she has failed Jordan and the Republic miserably.

You learn something about Pilar here. Pablo may have discarded illusions about the cause long ago. And Jordan may be swiftly moving in the direction of losing his. But to Pilar, the ideal of the Republic is still very real. At first Jordan is upset with her. Then he realizes that he cannot afford "the luxury of being bitter." He says he'll find other ways to detonate the explosives. "It is nothing."

He has to improvise the detonation of a major demolition with makeshift materials, and he has to come up with the ideas for it within a few hours. Considering the situation, Jordan's remarkably calm.

CHAPTER 34

Suspense builds in this chapter as Jordan prepares to carry off his mission with improvised explosive devices and Andrés moves to warn General Golz.

On his way to deliver Jordan's message to Golz,

Andrés looks at haystacks in a field, there since the beginning of the fighting. The hay is worthless now. Are the stacks symbolic of normal life in Spain right now, left to rot by the fighting? Being a true Republican, of course, Andrés blames it on the Nationalists with the ingrained slogan: "What barbarians they are!"

A partridge whirring at his feet prompts thoughts of what life could be like if there were no war: he could get the eggs and hatch partridges. His brother Eladio and he could gather crayfish. Life could be good without the war.

His pastoral musings turn more philosophical. Why is he on this side in the war? Because his father was. If his father's political views had been different, he and Eladio would be fascists!

NOTE: Inherited loyalties vs. independent thinking Have you inherited any loyalties? For example, do you favor one political party or another basically because your parents did? Unthinking acceptance of anything and everything simply because Mom or Dad said so is not the hallmark of an independent adult. But should parents deliberately *not* try to transmit values they consider important? That hardly seems right either. The reflections of Andrés can help us think about this ever-present dilemma. How far should parents go in trying to instill values in children?

CHAPTER 35

Maria is asleep. Jordan is furious with himself for not remembering to be on guard when he saw

Pablo's friendliness, the sign of imminent betrayal. The exploder and the detonators will be hard to replace with improvised materials. In fact, the whole operation may now be impossible. Jordan flies into a rage in which he attacks everything, particularly Spain and Spaniards.

But after realizing he is being unjust, his anger fades. He says to a still-sleeping Maria that he's figured out how to improvise the detonation. And then he echoes Pilar by saying, "We'll be killed but we'll blow the bridge." He considers Maria as his wife, and his wedding present is that she has been able to sleep this night without worrying.

The chapter ends with Robert Jordan the soldier counting the minutes until the offensive begins, while Robert Jordan the lover holds Maria close to him.

CHAPTER 36

Andrés is having his problems—but not with the enemy. He made it through their lines with ease. His problem is with Republican soldiers at their checkpoint.

He can't convince them that he's on their side and that he's carrying an important message for General Golz. Of course, they can't be blamed for being skeptical, for enforcing a sensible degree of security. But that's not what they're really doing. One soldier suggests tossing a bomb at him as "the soundest way to deal with the whole thing."

Andrés has encounterd some of the radical anarchists fighting for the Republic. In a sense they're little boys playing at war. As long as they destroy something or somebody (it makes little difference what), they feel they've accomplished something.

By mouthing some anarchist slogans, Andrés manages to get to them without being shot. The bomb advocate then becomes maudlin, embraces Andrés, and says he's "very content" that nothing happened to his "brother."

After more bumbling scrutiny, the officer agrees to lead the way to the commander. After Andrés has been walking behind him in the dark for several minutes, the officer belatedly decides it might be a good idea to take the gun from Andrés, whom he still doesn't completely trust. With such soldiers on the side of the Republic, no wonder Jordan is depressed.

CHAPTER 37

In Chapter 37, Jordan and Maria share an episode of lovemaking that touches each of them to the center of their being.

Examine the paragraph that begins, "Then they were together . . . " Some readers think it tries to parallel the rise and fall of intensity during lovemaking itself. Beyond question, it lyrically enforces Hemingway's idea of the meaning and value of the present moment.

Jordan displays a humility you may find surprising. He thanks Maria, not just for their lovemaking but for having taught him so much. Jordan, the college professor, admits that he really didn't know much about life until he came here. Now at least he has learned a few things.

CHAPTER 38

This chapter offers several surprises. We see Jordan in an unusual mood, and the expedition to blow up the bridge gets a strange boost from—of all people—Pablo.

It's 2:50 A.M. on his fourth day when Robert Jordan enters the cave. Pilar is attending to breakfast, and the men are generally irritable. Jordan is too, now that the time has come. Looking over his resources, he doesn't think the operation can work. There aren't enough men to take both the posts at the bridge. He's angry with many things, including himself for having spent the night with Maria instead of scouring the countryside for additional volunteers.

Pilar tries to reassure him that all will go well, and adds, "It is for this that we are born." Joaquín, you will remember, was saying similar things up until his last moments.

Then Pablo enters the cave. His explanation for leaving? He had had a moment of weakness but couldn't stand the loneliness of being a deserter. With him he's brought five volunteers and their horses. Unfortunately, he hasn't brought the exploder and the detonators. He threw them into the river during his moment of weakness.

Pilar alternately welcomes him and compares him to Judas. As for Pablo, he doesn't grovel; he doesn't even ask for forgiveness. He does, of course, ask for a drink.

They're ready to begin the operation.

CHAPTER 39

The band is on its way. Pablo seems worried about two things: the horses needed for the retreat and the fact that the men he's recruited think *he* is in charge. Jordan humors him on both counts.

NOTE: Jordan makes two religious allusions (to conversion and canonizing) in reference to Pablo's return. He compares it to the conversion of Paul on the road to Damascus (Acts 9:1–9). (Hemingway incorrectly cites Tarsus, Paul's birthplace, as the destination when the conversion occurred.) Canonization is the process in the Roman Catholic church by which a deceased person is declared a saint.

On the way to the bridge, Jordan muses on the idea that he himself is nothing, death is nothing. On the other hand, he has now learned that he plus another person could be everything.

But that's the exception, he tells himself. And even though the exception has happened, he can't afford to think about it now. The qualities of Jordan the lover—gentleness and sentimentality, for instance—apparently will not serve the needs of Jordan the soldier.

CHAPTER 40

This chapter is another installment in the story of Andrés as he is hampered by his own people. You will remember he had made swift progress through enemy territory. It's his own people who still continue to slow him down.

Again, if one of Hemingway's goals in *For Whom the Bell Tolls* was to show that a noble cause died at the hands of self-interested leaders, this chapter is one of his most successful, devastating efforts.

The scene is populated by selfish and short-sighted military men.

First there's the pompous, suspicious company commander who escorts Andrés to battalion headquarters. Then there's the self-important Gomez, a former barber now a battalion commander, who insists on personally driving Andrés to brigade headquarters. Finally, there's Lieutenant-Colonel Miranda, whose only ambition is to finish the war with the same rank. He is supported in this vital role by whiskey, sodium bicarbonate, cigarettes, and a pregnant mistress.

Miranda issues official clearance papers for Andrés and asks Gomez to take Andrés on his motorcycle to General Golz.

CHAPTER 41

The operation begins in the dark of early morning. The band has arrived at the bridge and is about to break up into various details.

As they shake hands in parting, Pablo's hand feels strangely good to Jordan, as though he were a real comrade.

With Pilar, Jordan trades some genial insults.

With Maria, the good-bye is awkward. As Jordan bends to give her a final kiss, his pack filled with war materials bumps the back of his head and makes his forehead bump hers. Other than that, their farewell is pared to the bone: "Good-bye, rabbit." "Good-bye, my Roberto."

Pablo and his five men have assumed the job El Sordo's band would have done. They leave to take care of the post on the other side of the bridge. As Jordan, Agustín and Anselmo start down the hill, they review their plans. Anselmo will go to the other side of the bridge to set the detonation assembly there. Jordan will shoot the sentry at this end of the bridge. Anselmo is then to do the same at his end. Agustín is to cover them both. Jordan again gives Anselmo instructions at what part of the man's body to aim, depending upon the man's position.

To remove some of Anselmo's guilt about killing, Jordan makes it clear that he is *ordering* it. Thus Anselmo can say to himself that he was only following orders. The orders came from a leader of the cause; the cause is right and good. Therefore, Anselmo did not do a bad thing; at least he cannot be held responsible. Jordan's sensitivity to the old man's plight is a further indication that his understanding of those around him has increased considerably in the course of the novel.

CHAPTER 42

This second-to-last chapter drives home the incompetence and futility that have characterized the cause for which Robert Jordan is risking his life and his newly discovered future with Maria.

The Republican offensive is moving through the night in one direction as Gomez carries Andrés on his motorcycle in the other direction toward headquarters. Hemingway paints a scene like a slapstick sequence from an old silent movie. One truck rams into the rear of another at a control point, creating a massive bottleneck. Truck after truck in the convoy pulls up and stops so close to the one in front of it that none can move, and the smashed vehicle in the original accident can't be removed from the road. An officer tries to run to the end of the line to tell the last truck to back up—but trucks keep arriving faster than he can run, and the end of the line moves farther away from him.

The mighty Republican army is on the move, so to speak. Its big top-secret offensive is getting in gear!

But Andrés rides past this ridiculous confusion in childlike hero worship. "Look at the army that has been builded!" he thinks exultantly to himself.

Finally, after some more delays, they arrive at headquarters. Just then a staff car pulls up and out of it steps a man whom Gomez recognizes: the famous André Marty! This legendary leader will certainly get the message through to Golz without any more red tape. So Gomez thinks as Marty reads the dispatch.

Instead, Marty has them arrested.

What Gomez doesn't know is that the great Comrade Marty has become an incompetent shell of a leader. He is inclined to execute people he thinks are traitors. Even the corporal refers to André Marty as "the crazy."

Hemingway gives us a brilliant picture of the tortured reasoning in what's left of André Marty's mind. Marty decides from their story that Golz is a traitor and that this is really a fascist communication.

We learn later that Marty often doesn't even understand the war maps he "studies." He simply points a finger and gives directions. His puppets agree and dispatch troops to their death carrying out his militarily absurd orders.

NOTE: André Marty Marty was a real historical character, a French communist who commanded the International Brigades in the Spanish Civil War. Hemingway felt contempt for him in real life and paints him as uncomplimentarily as possible in *For Whom the Bell Tolls*.

Many people agreed with Hemingway's opinion of Marty. But not all. After *For Whom the Bell Tolls* was published, an open letter to Hemingway bearing several signatures accused him of libeling Marty (and La Pasionaria). It didn't, of course, change Hemingway's opinion. He wrote a particularly bitter reply to one of the signers saying, "You have your Marty [André Marty] and I've married my Marty [Martha Gellhorn, his third wife and a noted writer] and we'll see who does the most for the world in the end."

Karkov, the Soviet journalist, shows up (through the efforts of the corporal) to save Gomez and Andrés. There's a dramatic battle of words (and relative status) between Karkov and Marty, but the Soviet is one of the few people not intimidated by the supposedly legendary figure.

Karkov wins. Gomez and Andrés are released. It's nearing daybreak now.

Jordan's dispatch goes to Duval, Golz's chief of staff, but he doesn't have sufficient authority or information to cancel the attack. However, he doesn't want to send men to their death if the offensive is expected by the enemy. Finally, he is able to contact Golz and transmit Jordan's message. Now you learn the truth. The attack is not a holding action. It's the real thing.

But the huge offensive the Republic has mounted will find no targets. The enemy won't be where they were supposed to be. They've heard. They've gone from the slopes and the ridges. Instead they'll be waiting for the attackers.

But nothing can stop the orders. There will be tragedy . . . and many dead Loyalist soldiers.

Golz, in the very moment he receives the news, looks up at his planes beginning the unstoppable, futile, destined-to-be disastrous attack. He sees his thundering, silvery-gleaming power streaking across the sky, and he's proud of how it *could* and *should* have been.

Hemingway has spent a great deal of time leading up to the following, final chapter. In it, Robert Jordan and a makeshift band of peasant volunteers will attempt to blow up a bridge behind enemy lines.

Before you read or reread this final chapter, think of how Hemingway has prepared you for it. How is it different from the climax of other war and/or adventure stories you have read? What's at stake in this story besides the victory in a test of military expertise?

Are you resentful that Jordan has to do this at all? Do you wish you could call out to him and say, "Stop! It isn't worth it!"? Are you angry that Jordan is still doggedly pursuing his "duty," even though it now seems a waste? Or do you feel that he put himself in the situation, so it's his problem and he must accept whatever happens? In either case, do you see his actions as noble and honorable?

CHAPTER 43

The final, lengthy chapter of *For Whom the Bell Tolls* is devoted almost exclusively to action. Hemingway has completed his philosophizing. He now leaves it to you to gather the thematic threads and weave them into the story's final scenes as you learn the fate of the bridge, of the guerrilla band, and of Robert Jordan.

As Jordan sets out to blow up the bridge, he knows that the Republican offensive is unlikely to be successful. Subconsciously, he's known that for quite some time, and he now admits it. He admits that victory for the cause is several years away. It can't be expected with this bridge, this offensive. It'll take better equipment for one thing. Portable short-wave radios would have helped in this particular operation, he muses. But he's going to give this operation his all anyway, since what will happen in the future can depend on what is done today. How do you feel about his attitude? You might compare your feelings going into an activity that you were virtually positive would not be successful. Did you try your best to succeed despite the odds? Or did you simply try to avoid getting hurt or totally disgraced—and then wait for "next time?"

Jordan watches the changing of the sentries at each end of the bridge. He sees the new sentry at his end, sleepy and rolling a cigarette. Jordan decides he won't look at him again.

Even here, Hemingway raises the theme of the individual person. Why won't Jordan look again at the sentry? Maybe he doesn't care to see the man as a man like himself, not simply as "one of them." That would be extremely uncomfortable. It might make him hesitate. At this point, Jordan the soldier cannot afford to hesitate.

He hears the bombs—the signal for him to begin.

The sentry hears them too, stands up, and comes out of his sentry box. It's the last thing he does; Jordan is a very good shot. Anselmo, at the other end of the bridge, has done his job too, although not quite as coldly. The big difference, when they meet at the center, is that Anselmo has tears for what he's done. Jordan doesn't, but notices Anselmo's tears and remarks to himself, "Goddam good face." The old man is left to comfort himself very briefly with, "We *have* to kill them."

It's time for Jordan the demolition expert to prove his stuff. And he does. Remember he has to improvise, because Pablo threw out the detonation devices.

But what does he think of while he's hanging on the bridge, improvising a way to blow it up and bring victory to the great cause? His mind leaps from one subject to the next—Anselmo's killing of the enemy soldier, a trout in the water below, the colors of the hillside. He even plays word games as he associates his name with that of the Jordan River and the old hymn, "Roll, Jordan roll." He cautions himself to "pull yourself together." Hemingway captures very well the intense pressure Jordan must be undergoing as he waits for whatever will happen next.

In the meantime, two of the band will not see the hillside turn completely green. Eladio has been shot in the head. Fernando is lying fatally wounded on the hillside. Hemingway paints a moving picture of Fernando's loyalty and willingness to serve even to the death.

Pilar is becoming impatient with Jordan's slowness in bringing about the actual demolition. Jordan himself isn't too happy with its progress and wishes there were more time. He's playing out more wire toward the opposite end of the bridge when he hears firing from that end.

He wishes it were Pablo, but it isn't. It's the Nationalists. Jordan is desperate for time now. He needs only a few more seconds. He hears the truck coming; then he sees it; then he shouts to Anselmo, "Blow her!"

". . . and then it commenced to rain pieces of steel."

The aftermath: the center section of the bridge is gone. So is Anselmo, killed by a piece of steel from the blast. Fernando on the nearby hillside is unconscious, with little life left.

Pilar congratulates Jordan, but he is in no mood for congratulations. Hemingway has an explanation for this: "In him, too, was despair from the sorrow that soldiers turn to hatred in order that they may continue to be soldiers." Sorrow to despair to hatred . . . so that the cycle can continue.

Then the scene shifts to Maria, as she holds the horses for the retreat. She follows the pattern of Joaquín and Anselmo: when danger is imminent (in this case, as she sees it, more to Jordan than to herself), she prays—"automatically," Hemingway tells us.

It's the type of prayer sometimes called a bartering with God. She promises (in this case the Virgin Mary) she'll do "anything thou sayest ever" as long as Jordan returns safe from the bridge.

And then the bridge explodes.

Pilar shouts to her that her "*Inglés*" is all right.

Watching the planes in the sky, Jordan knows

that things are going wrong, and he feels a sense of unreality. Four days ago everything was okay. He was the American *partizan*, here to do a demolition for the sake of the Republicans just as he had done several times before. Now he almost can't comprehend what he's become involved in.

Look at the line "It was as though you had thrown a stone and the stone made a ripple and the ripple returned roaring and toppling as a tidal wave." This image, and those that immediately follow— the echo, the striking of one man—emphasize Hemingway's theme of interdependency. Just as one act on Jordan's part has resulted in a number of other acts that affect all those around him, so the actions of everyone affect many other people. What may seem minor can have a monumental impact.

Pablo reappears, scrambling across the bridge-less gorge. There will be plenty of horses now, he announces. All of his recently recruited volunteers are dead. He has killed them for their horses so that his original band of guerrillas can escape. His justification for shooting? "They were not of our band."

Jordan and Maria share a limited but intense reunion at the scene of the horses Maria had been watching.

It's time for the escape. Pablo has the plan: they will ride down the slope to the road and cross it one at a time. Crossing the road will be dangerous because they'll be within range of the enemy tank up by the bridge. But it's the only way. After they have crossed the road and ridden up into the timber of the opposite slope, they can head for the Gredos Mountains and safety.

Pablo and the others, including Maria, make the crossing. They draw fire but make it safely. Jordan makes it across the road too. Then, as his horse is laboring up the slope, there's "a banging acrid smelling clang like a boiler being ripped apart."

The enemy tank has had a lucky shot. Aiming into the timber, it has found a target—but not Robert Jordan. His horse has been hit and has fallen on him. In the fall, Jordan's thigh is so badly broken that the leg swivels in all directions like a piece of loose string. The broken edge of the bone is nearly through the skin.

Primitivo and Agustín drag him further up to safety. Pilar assures him that they can bind up the injury and he can ride one of the pack horses. But Pablo shakes his head—meaning it won't work. Jordan can't ride the horse and make it. Jordan nods agreement.

Pablo is a realist now. Has he, in fact, been the realist all along? In spite of his weakness for wine, horses, and a relatively comfortable life at the hideout, has he seen some things more clearly than the other people have?

Jordan and Pablo converse briefly. Both are aware of the crucial shortage of time. Both know that Jordan and Maria must say a final good-bye. But Maria will not want to leave her man behind. Jordan instructs Pablo on how to handle her.

"We will not be going to Madrid," he tells Maria.

Of course they won't. But how long have you known or suspected that Jordan and Maria's "storybook" romance would not be a "lived happily ever after" tale of a college professor and his lovely Spanish wife?

Maria will not leave until he commands her to

do so. He explains that he will live on in her, that he will go on to Madrid in her: "Thou art all there will be of me."

Pilar and Pablo take her away. A final time, just before she disappears from sight, she begs to stay, and again he repeats, "I am with thee . . . We are both there."

The last of the band to say good-bye is Agustín. Even this hardened, foul-mouthed peasant is crying. He asks if Jordan wants to be shot. Jordan declines. He will stay there on the hillside with the one small machine gun and try to be useful.

NOTE: As he lies there, Jordan's mind wanders through a variety of subjects: the past three days, his life in general, his grandfather, the fate of his comrades now fleeing to another retreat. As he tries to endure the increasing pain, he even allows a bit of humor to enter his thoughts, as he wishes briefly that he had brought a spare leg.

Throughout the interior monologue, the central theme that emerges is "No man is an iland." Jordan has chosen to stay behind and serve as a temporary obstacle to the approaching enemy in order to help the others, especially Maria. At one point he says to himself, "You can do nothing for yourself, but perhaps you can do something for another." In that simple statement, Jordan reveals that he has moved from thinking mainly about the Republican cause to thinking about the well-being of another individual.

The cause is still important, to be sure, but it now shares a place in his heart and his consciousness with the realization that human beings are

equally as important. The fate of one man is inter-
locked with the fate of others.

With immense effort, Jordan manages to turn
his body over and around so that he's lying on his
belly, facing downhill, in a position to be "useful"
with his machine gun when the enemy appears on
the road below.

The broken leg, which had been almost numb
at first, now begins to pain Jordan terribly and brings
the prospect of suicide to mind. He weighs the
reasons for and against it. Basically, it seems cowardly and reminds him of his father.

But several times he feels himself losing consciousness from the pain. If enemy soldiers find
him unconscious, they will revive him and probably torture him to gain information. That possibility seems to make suicide the lesser of two evils.

Again and again he changes his mind. Suicide
would be acceptable . . . then, no it wouldn't—not
as long as there's something left that you can do.

He keeps hanging on and hoping the enemy will
come soon. And they do. Hemingway says that
Robert Jordan's luck held very good. The Nationalist soldiers are on the trail of Pablo and his band.
Holding them up or causing confusion by killing
the officer is one final thing Jordan can do. But this
time it's not so much to aid the Republic. It's to
buy time for Maria and the others.

The officer comes into view. In a final piece of
irony, it's Lieutenant Berrendo—the man who didn't
climb El Sordo's hill because he was positive someone was alive up there. He will pass within twenty
yards of Robert Jordan.

Robert Jordan lies, just as he did in the opening scene of the story, on the pine-needled forest floor of the Spanish mountains.

NOTE: At first, Hemingway was somewhat dissatisfied with the ending of the book at Chapter 43, and wrote an epilogue of two short chapters. One featured a meeting between Karkov and Golz in which they discussed, among other things, Jordan's blowing up the bridge and his disappearance. The other described Andrés returning to the former hideout of Pablo's band, where he gazes down at the wrecked bridge. Later Hemingway decided these chapters were unnecessary.

A STEP BEYOND

Tests and Answers

TESTS

Test 1

1. Robert Jordan became involved in the ____
   Spanish Civil War because of his
   A. inborn sense of adventure
   B. philosophical and political views
   C. need to find meaning in a superficial
      lifestyle

2. One of the powerful themes of *For Whom* ____
   the Bell Tolls is
   A. the importance of the individual
   B. the triumph of fascism
   C. readiness is all

3. In Robert Jordan's opinion, the most ____
   trustworthy of Pablo's band was
   A. Rafael   B. Primitivo
   C. Anselmo

4. Robert Jordan's growth and character ____
   change stem from
   A. his interaction with people
   B. different philosophical viewpoints he
      encounters
   C. disappointment with his previous life

5. Robert Jordan feels ____

   A. admiration for the Spanish people
   B. disgust for the Spanish people
   C. at different times, each of the above

6. The reactions of Joaquín, Anselmo, and _____
Maria, when confronted with the strong
possibility of death, show that
   A. they are superficial, hypocritical
      people
   B. the atheism of the Republicans has
      not really destroyed their faith
   C. they believe that sincere religion will
      win the war for the Republic

7. At the beginning of *For Whom the Bell Tolls*, _____
Robert Jordan sees blowing up the bridge
as
   A. simply another operation to be
      accomplished
   B. the crowning glory of his career with
      the Republicans
   C. an omen of bad things to come

8. Which of the following relationships began _____
with distrust but ended with mutual con-
fidence?
   A. Jordan and General Golz
   B. Jordan and Maria
   C. Jordan and Pablo

9. How is Robert Jordan's relationship with Maria different from the relationships he has had with other
women?

10. Sketch the change in Robert Jordan's views about
the Republicans and fighting for them.

11. Is Pablo a villain or a hero in *For Whom the Bell Tolls*?

Test 2

1. The attempt of Andrés to deliver Jordan's   ____
   letter to Golz brings out the
   A. dedication of the Loyalist peasants
   B. unfeeling cruelty of both sides in the
      war
   C. incompetence of the Republican
      military

2. The character associated with mysticism and   ____
   fatalism is
   A. Pilar   B. Maria   C. Pablo

3. Which of the following is a key moral issue   ____
   in *For Whom the Bell Tolls*?
   A. How can something be necessary and
      evil at the same time?
   B. Is it possible to love one's enemies?
   C. Should love of a single person be
      stronger than love of all people?

4. The Republican attempt to take Segovia fails   ____
   mainly because
   A. Jordan's bridge demolition was badly
      timed
   B. key supplies did not reach the forces
      in time
   C. Nationalist forces had learned of the
      planned attack

5. El Sordo and his band were killed   ____
   A. because they tried to take the bridge
      demolition into their own hands

B. in an attempt to help Jordan and
Pablo's band
C. through the deceit and treachery of
Pablo

6. At one point, Pablo's band decide he should ____
be killed because
A. they could not tolerate his cruel
dictatorship
B. his current emotional state was
dangerous to the band's operations
C. it was obvious he was about to sell
out to the enemy

7. Jordan tries to reconcile Maria to their final ____
parting by
A. promising to meet her in Madrid
B. deliberately being cold and unfeeling
so she will resent rather than miss
him
C. telling her that he will live on in her
being and her life

8. At the end of *For Whom the Bell Tolls*, Robert ____
Jordan is
A. bitter about the way his life is about
to end
B. relatively content with how things
have turned out
C. so confused he does not know what
to think

9. Is *For Whom the Bell Tolls* an antiwar novel?

10. Cite instances of irony in *For Whom the Bell Tolls*.

11. Explain the significance of the novel's title.

ANSWERS

Test 1

1. B   **2.** A   **3.** C   **4.** A   **5.** C   **6.** B
7. A   **8.** C

9. It's obvious that Robert Jordan's relationship with Maria is more meaningful to him than relationships he's had with other women. But this extends beyond his enjoyment of sex or even small talk. We're given only a shallow description—just a line or two—of his previous relationships. Perhaps that indicates they were insignificant.

Maria, however, is very special. She makes him think; she helps him grow. Maria causes him to see people, not just ideas, politics, and ideology. We get the impression that previous women in his life were more like objects that he didn't always have time for in spite of their attractiveness. But he appreciates Maria as a person, not merely as an object. Consequently, he is able to see *himself* as a person—not merely as a warrior on behalf of a political idea.

10. It's possible to defend two different but not completely opposite positions on this matter. On the one hand, Jordan has admitted by his own words that he no longer completely believes in the theories that originally brought him to the war—and hasn't for some time. Toward the end he says that love is all that really counts. He seems to discredit what he previously knew in favor of what he's learned. Thus he seems to have done a complete turnaround.

But you may find some passages, even toward the end, which don't support the complete turnaround idea. For example, if he had truly abandoned his loyalty to the Republic in favor of loyalty to Maria, wouldn't he have found a safe way to leave and take her with him? Long after Maria and others have made an impression on him, he's concerned about being the kind of soldier that would make his grandfather proud. Thus it could be argued that he has changed his priorities intellectually, but in practice he's not ready to abandon everything he previously championed.

11. Pablo is perhaps the most complex character in *For Whom the Bell Tolls,* so you can make a case for either hero or villain. Perhaps your choice will depend upon how you see him at the end.

Certainly his brief desertion caused harm. Jordan says that Anselmo would still be alive if the makeshift exploders hadn't required him to be so close to the bridge. Throughout the operation, Pablo's instability is a constant source of tension and worry. He's frequently drunk or nearly so. Even before he "went bad," one of his glories was the engineering of an incredibly brutal mass execution.

Yet, Pablo did return after leaving with the detonator and the exploders. For many people, this would not have been easy. He worked out an escape plan and seems to be in charge again as the group leave Jordan on the hillside. Many readers feel that under Pablo's renewed leadership the band will make it to safety. (Of course, they have enough horses to do so because Pablo murdered his five newly recruited peasant volunteers.)

Test 2
1. C   **2.** A   **3.** A   **4.** C   **5.** B   **6.** B
7. C   **8.** B

9. Beyond question, Hemingway presents one human tragedy after another in *For Whom the Bell Tolls.* Think of all the things that could be described as a waste. The loss of life, including Jordan's, is wasted in the sense that the deaths do nothing to advance the cause. Even the demolition of the bridge, the central event of the story, turns out to be wasted effort. The common people, on whose behalf the war is supposed to be waged, do not really want it and seem unlikely to benefit from it. You should have no trouble finding things that are wasted as a result of the war.

Yet these things concern a particular war, so you may find it questionable that the book is an attack on war in general. Furthermore, it could be argued that some good things do come from it. The war brings Jordan and Maria together. The war brings Jordan in contact with all the people who change his life and foster his growth as a person.

10. Skimming through the story should provide you with many instances of irony, which is a situation or an outcome of events opposite to what might logically be expected. It's ironic in a general sense that the "good guys" (the Loyalist forces) in the conflict are also often incompetent fools. Also, the most competent Loyalist leaders in this "civil" war are foreigners.

The prayers of Anselmo, Joaquín, and Maria are ironic against the background of the movement's official atheism. Anselmo and Lieutenant Berrendo's uttering of the very same prayer is a telling example. The horse that was Jordan's means of escape prevents his escape when it falls on him. And the war itself, which ultimately killed Robert Jordan, was also the occasion of his truly appreciating life and other people.

11. The title is taken from John Donne's well-known poem, published in 1624, which begins, "No man is an *Iland* . . . ." The poem itself makes the point that all human life is interconnected, and whatever happens to even one person affects all humanity. Thus with each individual's death, a little bit of every other person "dies." When you hear the tolling of the church bell, therefore, don't send to ask for whom the bell tolls—it tolls for thee.

You may or may not agree with this idea, but look for examples of it in the novel. Certainly Jordan's parting words to Maria—that he will live on in her—are a direct illustration. And certainly a part of her will die because of Jordan's death and their separation.

El Sordo refers to the Nationalist captain he kills as Comrade Voyager. Each will have caused the other's death, either directly or indirectly, and they are journeying to death together.

Still another example comes from Anselmo's reflections that the fascist soldiers they "have to" kill are individual men just like himself. A little bit of his own principles is destroyed each time he kills.

Term Paper Ideas and other Topics for Writing

Robert Jordan

1. Does Jordan's death—shortly after he's discovered so much to live for—make him a genuinely tragic figure? Has he in some way contributed to his own death?

2. "Jordan's involvement in the war is due merely to his infatuation with an ideology." Tell why you agree or disagree with that statement.

3. How is Robert Jordan a genuinely better person as a

result of his rather brief experience with the resistance band?

Other Characters

1. Pablo is sometimes called the most complex of the characters in the novel. What supports this view?

2. Some readers feel that Maria is not a developed character in the novel but a cardboard figure or a symbol of women in general. True or false?

3. Which character does Hemingway portray the most sympathetically? which the most unsympathetically?

4. Does Pilar herself believe in palm reading? Is she completely honest when she says she reads palms just to get attention? Do her actions give evidence for one interpretation more than the other?

War

1. Is war by itself wrong? When is it justified?

2. Do foreign countries have the right to aid one side or another in a civil war? Is there any similarity between the situation of the Spanish Civil War and the situation in Indochina after 1954?

Idealism

1. What were the ideals of the Spanish Republic, and were these ideals sufficient to justify a terrible war?

2. Is idealism always naive? Try to cite some examples where "pure" idealism has been immensely practical— or try to show that this is seldom or never the case.

Integrity/Hypocrisy

1. Did Jordan's political idealism cause him to compromise his honesty and self-respect? Which of his actions, if any, could be called hypocritical?

2. Anselmo kills against his will and feels tremendous guilt. Does this make him a hypocrite? How is he, in spite of that, an example of integrity?

Religion
1. Were there any truly atheistic characters in the book? Which ones?

2. *For Whom the Bell Tolls* has been called "a mockery of faith and religion." Write in support of, or against, this viewpoint.

Further Reading
CRITICAL WORKS

Astro, Richard, and Jackson Benson. *Hemingway in Our Time.* Corvallis: Oregon State University Press, 1974.

Baker, Carlos. *Ernest Hemingway: A Life Story.* New York: Scribner's, 1969. Generally considered the definitive biography of Hemingway.

———. *Hemingway: The Writer as Artist.* 3d ed. Princeton: Princeton University Press, 1963.

Burgess, Anthony. *Ernest Hemingway and His World.* New York: Scribner's, 1978.

Griffin, Peter. *Along With Youth: Hemingway, the Early Years.* New York: Oxford University Press, 1985. Biography; also includes five previously unpublished early short stories by Hemingway.

Hotchner, A. E. *Papa Hemingway: The Ecstasy and Sorrow.* New York: William Morrow, 1983.

Laurence, Frank M. *Hemingway and the Movies.* Jackson: University Press of Mississippi, 1981.

Meyers, Jeffrey. *Hemingway: A Biography.* New York: Harper & Row, 1985.

———. *Hemingway: The Critical Heritage*. London: Routledge and Kegan Paul, 1982.

Nagel, James, ed. *Ernest Hemingway: The Writer in Context*. Madison: University of Wisconsin Press, 1984.

Noble, Donald R., ed. *Hemingway: A Revaluation*. Troy, N.Y.: Whitson Publishing Company, 1983.

Rao, E. Nageswara. *Ernest Hemingway: A Study of His Rhetoric*. Atlantic Highlands, N.J.: Humanities Press, 1983.

Rovit, Earl. *Ernest Hemingway*. New York: Twayne, 1963.

Weeks, Robert P., ed. *Hemingway: A Collection of Critical Essays*. Englewood Cliffs, N.J.: Prentice-Hall, 1972.

Williams, Wirt. *The Tragic Art of Ernest Hemingway*. Baton Rouge: Louisiana State University Press, 1981.

Wylder, Delbert E. *Hemingway's Heroes*. Albuquerque: University of New Mexico Press, 1969.

AUTHOR'S OTHER MAJOR WORKS

1925	*In Our Time*
1926	*The Torrents of Spring*
1926	*The Sun Also Rises*
1927	*Men Without Women*
1929	*A Farewell to Arms*
1932	*Death in the Afternoon*
1933	*Winner Take Nothing*
1935	*Green Hills of Africa*
1937	*To Have and Have Not*
1938	*The Fifth Column, and The First Forty-Nine Stories*
1942	*Men at War*
1950	*Across the River and Into the Trees*
1952	*The Old Man and the Sea*
1962	*A Moveable Feast*
1972	*Islands in the Stream*

The Critics

A Negative View

Hemingway's novel is Tolstoyan in scope but rarely in achievement. But it has many merits, and even its defects are generally interesting . . . Yet the novel falls considerably short of greatness. To some extent, Hemingway's failure in his longest, most densely populated novel is stylistic, but far more serious are his distortions of the experience he describes. Together these technical and thematic flaws confuse and mislead the reader and, at last, diminish the novel.

—*Arthur Waldhorn*, A Reader's
Guide to Hemingway, *1972*

A Positive View

The result is a novel that is complex, meaningful, and as close to aesthetic perfection as Hemingway could make it. *For Whom the Bell Tolls* . . . stands somewhat in relation to Hemingway's other works as *Moby Dick* does to the rest of Melville's work. And, like *Moby Dick*, it is true enough to stand continued reinterpretation. . . .

The skill with which this novel was for the most part written demonstrated that Hemingway's talent was once again intact and formidable. None of his books had evoked more richly the life of the senses, had shown a truer sense of plotting, or provided more fully living secondary characters, or livelier dialog.

—*Delbert E. Wylder*, Hemingway's
Heroes, *1969*

On the Bridge in *For Whom the Bell Tolls*

The brilliance of execution becomes apparent when the reader stands in imagination on the flooring of the bridge and looks in any direction. He will see his horizons lifting by degrees towards a circumference far beyond the Guadarrama mountains. For the guerrillas' central task, the blowing of the bridge, is only one phase of a larger operation which Hemingway once called "the greatest holding action in history." Since the battle strategy which requires the bridge to be destroyed is early made available to the reader, he has no difficulty in seeing its relation to the next circle outside, where a republican division under General Golz prepares for an attack. The general's attack, in turn, is enough to suggest the outlines of the whole civil war, while the Heinkel bombers and Fiat pursuit planes which cut across the circle—foreign shadows over the Spanish earth—extend our grasp one more circle outwards to the trans-European aspect of the struggle. The outermost ring of the circle is nothing less than the great globe itself. Once the Spanish holding operation is over, the wheel of fire will encompass the earth. The bridge, therefore—such is the structural achievement of this novel—becomes the hub on which the "future of the human race can turn."

—*Carlos Baker*, Hemingway: The
Writer as Artist, *1963*

On Sex and Love in the Novel

It is not surprising that sex becomes more dominant the deeper one gets beneath the outer political surface of the novel, since it is the sexual experience with Maria that is the basis of Jordan's mystical experience.

—*Delbert E. Wylder*, Hemingway's
Heroes, *1969*

The nadir [of *For Whom the Bell Tolls*] is the love

scenes. Possibly it is these that set up initial hostility to the book in some critics. These scenes fail because Hemingway not only breaks but reverses a principle that served him so well in earlier works: to undercut anything to do with romantic love so sharply that even the possibility of sentimentality is extinguished.

> —*Wirt Williams*, The Tragic Art of
> Ernest Hemingway, *1981*

On the Novel and the Spanish People

Devoted to the Loyalist cause, Hemingway remains sufficiently the objective artist to delineate the human faults of what the left-wing propagandists wished to see presented as an incorrupt and shining chivalry. *For Whom the Bell Tolls* is not propaganda but art, and like all art it promotes a complex, even ambivalent, attachment to its subject. The book taught thousands to love or hate Spain, but it could not leave them indifferent to the land, its people, its history.

> —*Anthony Burgess*, Ernest
> Hemingway and His World,
> *1978*

I myself was fascinated by the book and felt it to be honest in so far as it renders Hemingway's real vision. And yet I find myself awkwardly alone in the conviction that, as a novel about Spaniards and their war, it is unreal and, in the last analysis, deeply untruthful.

> —*Arturo Barea* (Spanish novelist)
> *in* Horizon, *1941*

NOTES

NOTES

NOTES